DEVIOUS LIES

JERSEY BAD BOYS
BOOK 2

C.D. GORRI

DEVIOUS LIES

Jersey Bad Boys
Book 2
By C.D. Gorri

Copyright C.D. Gorri, NJ 2024

Before you begin sign up for my newsletter here:
SUBSCRIBE HERE

DEDICATION

It's always the quiet ones you have to watch out for. The ones you least suspect. So, if your type runs towards the Phantom, Count Dracula, Killmonger, and more brilliantly brutal bad guys, keep reading. You're gonna enjoy this.

There's no room for mercy in a kingdom built on lies.

Beneath the veneer of polite society exists a criminal organization known for its utter lack of mercy. They call themselves the Vipers. The men who belong to this syndicate are cruel, cunning, and unforgiving. Ruled by a king, this band of brothers knows no boundaries and takes no prisoners. To cross them is to sign your own death certificate.

But even serpents have weaknesses.

And sometimes that weakness is just a flower.

Our Bad Boys:
Nico Fury
Luc Batiste
Angel Fury

Content Warnings:

This is a contemporary romance series of connected standalones, featuring familiar tropes such as enemies to lovers, forced proximity, arranged marriages, secret

They say two wrongs don't make a right. But what if they did?

Maria

It was always only a matter of time before my past would catch up with me. I knew it the second I lied on my job application, I was taking a huge risk. But anything was better than the crime family I was born into.

I knew I needed help, and I set my cap on the king only to be turned down. It was inevitable that someone from my old life was going to find me at the Vipers' Den.

I was ready for it, but I didn't expect him to step in. Luc Batiste, the Vipers' Council, was my savior. He wasn't loud and showy like the others. But it was always the quiet ones you had to watch out for. Now, I owed him my life. But he wanted the truth, and that was more than I could give.

Luc

There was something about her that never seemed to fit. Maria didn't belong behind a bar, slinging beers and booze.

She was too good for that. Too good for me. So, I kept my distance.

But I was there when that customer got a little too familiar, and there was no way I was going to let it go.

In my world, there are rules, and once a Viper claimed a woman, she was his. I just claimed Maria in the loudest way possible. She thought she could hide from me. That her secrets were safe. But they weren't.

Maria was mine now. That meant I owned every inch of her, including her past.

There was no getting away from it. No getting away from me. Sooner or later, Maria was going to have to accept it because I wasn't letting her go.

Devious Lies is the second in the contemporary

romance series of connected standalones, Jersey Bad Boys. This series features familiar tropes such as enemies to lovers, forced proximity, arranged marriages, secret babies, and contains some violence and explicit scenes.

PROLOGUE—MIA/MARIA

Six years ago...

S I smile as I join my mom in the kitchen. It smells delicious in here.

Like *pozole rojo*, and my mouth is watering.

It's my favorite soup, and she always makes it when I come home from school.

This break is longer because it's the end of the first semester and I'll be home through Christmas all the way through the Epiphany, and another week and a half after that.

In fact, I don't go back until January 17th.

"Mia! You snuck up on me," Mom says, and clutches her hand to her chest before turning to embrace me.

"Mami, I missed you," I tell her as I hug her back.

"I'm so glad you're home. Did you bring any laundry?"

I snort.

Of course, I did.

It's my fourth year at Monmouth University and though I'm still in New Jersey, the drive to Union City from campus is too long to commute. I walk to the small laundry room just off the kitchen in our tiny two-story house.

My father makes good money, and we're one of the few homeowners on our street. The others just rent.

I'm not sure what he does, but I know he works for the Sanchez family. Technically, we aren't related, but my dad and the head of their family come from the same small town in Mexico, so I grew up thinking they're our cousins.

Papi is a good man, regardless of what he does. He loves my mother and me and treats us with respect and kindness.

I'm lucky to have both my parents. Not a lot of girls I know from the neighborhood can say the same.

He is protective, though. He didn't want me to dorm, but he relented after I received a scholarship. I'll be the first one in my family to get a college degree, and my father's pride in me outweighs his overprotective fatherly instincts.

I'm studying English literature and having an excellent time doing it. I know it's not the kind of major that will make me a lot of money, but I don't know what I want to do yet.

Plus, I like reading.

"So, how are things?" Mami continues the conversation.

"Good," I tell her, and then I go on to chat about my roommate and finals.

After a little while, I help Mami cook. I've always loved helping in the kitchen since I was a kid.

I slice the radishes and limes, mincing cilantro and prepping all the toppings for the *pozole rojo*. She has a pot with homemade tamales simmering on the stove and I can smell pork roasting in the oven.

Dinner is going to be fantastic, and I can't wait. My mother isn't Mexican, but she learned to cook like a local for my father.

She's half Puerto Rican and half Italian and Irish. I suppose that makes me some kind of mutt, but that's New Jersey. Lots of immigrants have rolled through the Garden State over the last two hundred years and I'm proud of what I am.

I love having multiple ethnicities in my background. I was born Mia Alejandra Maria Lopez. It's a mouthful, but whatever. My father is Emiliano Lopez. My mother's name is Celia.

Papi works for Enrico Sanchez.

Why is that important?

It's important because my father is a soldier for the Sanchez cartel. More than that. He is a general, running his own battalion of soldiers, and his position is essential to the businessman's illegal empire.

Enrico Sanchez's reputation precedes him, though I only became aware of it recently.

I don't judge. The world is complicated and I don't understand it well enough to make assumptions.

I am very self aware for a woman my age and I know I can't begin to understand, and I should probably be scared of what it is my father does.

But I'm not.

I'm proud of my family.

Being at home is wonderful. I feel safe. Loved. And I can't wait for the holidays.

Okay, there's another reason I'm excited to have the next few weeks off from school.

I can't wait to see *him*.

I've met my father's boss on a handful of occasions. Most recently, when I came home from school to celebrate *el Día de los Muertos* a few weeks ago.

But he isn't who I want to see. It's his son.

Enrico Sanchez has three sons, but that celebration was the first time I actually met them.

The oldest, Junior, scares the hell out of me. Matteo is the middle one. He's hardly any better than Junior. But Carmine, the youngest, is an absolute dream.

The party was a lot of fun. And I had a great time.

The Sanchez villa is located on a private cul de sac in Montclair. Far away from where he conducts his business.

When I close my eyes, I can see the decorations and I smile. Thousands of candles, flowers, and *ofrendas* were set up.

Ofrendas are altars. Legend says they help guide the souls of the departed back to their families for this one night. This is my favorite part of my Mexican heritage.

That night, I felt like I was walking in a dream. There was food, music, and costumes. Most of all, there was magic. At least, that was how I felt when Carmine asked me to dance.

We've been texting, and I have to admit I like where it's going.

"Mia, where is your head? Don't you hear the front door?" Mami says, interrupting my reverie.

I feel my cheeks burn as I go to answer the door. But I couldn't have known what I would find on the other side.

Papi comes rushing in and he's got someone in his arms. More men follow and they're all shouting in Spanish.

I don't speak Spanish. Just a few words, clips, and phrases.

I gasp and step back.

"Mia, towels, quick!" Papi yells at me as he lays his burden on the couch.

That's when my stomach drops out.

It's Carmine. And he's been shot.

"No!" I sob and cover my mouth.

"Get a fucking towel, Bitch!"

Someone shoves me, and I turn and see Matteo.

He's bloody and bruised, but that doesn't seem to stop him from staring at my tits.

I back up.

"Hey! That's my daughter," Papi snarls.

I don't want them to fight, so I rush to do as he asks. Mami is by his side, and she looks scared and frantic.

There's so much blood, and between the cursing and shouting, I can hardly hear myself think.

I don't know what's going on, but I hear words like *trap, set up,* and *went bad.* It's enough for me to know something horrible happened.

"M-Mia," Carmine stutters my name and blood dribbles down his chin. He's gurgling and trying to reach for me, but I'm scared, frozen against the wall.

By the time the sun sets on Carmine, it's dark outside. I feel hollow. Empty.

Maybe it's shock.

I mean, the man I'd only kissed twice, who I only just started talking to really, is lying dead on my couch.

Sanchez sends a cleaner crew to come collect his dead son and the others who've been injured. They've been holed up in my parents' bedroom.

I don't miss the side-eye Junior gives my father. Or the leer Matteo directs at me when they leave.

I feel scared. And dirty.

My mother is scrubbing frantically at the ruined sofa, and my father pulls her away from her futile task. She sobs and he hugs her to his chest.

I've never seen fear in my father's eyes before, but I see it now. And it's gutting me.

"Papi?"

"Hush, *mija*. It will be alright."

PROLOGUE 2-MIA/MARIA

A few weeks later.

I'm standing outside in the cold with my mother sobbing beside me. It's January, the coldest month of the year in the Garden State.

The ground is almost too hard for the machinery to dig a proper grave. I feel numb. Alone. And scared.

My father is dead.

Just another statistic, killed in some random accident.

At least, that's what they told me and my mother. I can't help the thoughts in my head.

Enrico Sanchez and his two remaining sons are standing opposite me and my mother. He looks older, this man who has so much power.

Maybe the death of his favorite son is taking its toll.

I don't know. I am numb today.

They don't say anything.

Not exactly.

But it's the way Matteo keeps looking at me that leaves me uneasy.

My father is, *was*, a well-known man.

An important man.

That means the funeral is packed.

I tug my black coat tighter around me and shiver against the cold.

None of this feels real.

As we make our way from the graveside to the limo waiting for us, I help Mami inside first.

Then Enrico Sanchez steps in front of me.

"Allow me to accompany your mother, *nena*. We have much to discuss," he says.

I look at my mother, and she's almost catatonic.

I want to refuse, but I can't.

This man scares me.

I look around at the dozen or more soldiers in all black, their jackets bulging with what I can only guess are weapons, and I shiver.

No, I can't refuse him. He's the boss and I'm just the daughter of his dead general.

"You can ride with me," Matteo says, and before I can protest, Enrico Sanchez's son grabs my arm and tugs me towards a large blacked out SUV.

"Get in," he says with a slight shove.

I climb in.

I have no choice.

But I don't know what he will try to do on the short ride to my house.

I sit as close to the door as I can and try to make myself small.

Matteo is the kind of man who even though he is only five foot six, needs to feel big. I'm five foot nine.

I know this pisses him off.

"Look, Mia, I know you had feelings for Carmine, and I'm sorry for your loss," he says, but he sounds anything but sorry.

"Thank you," I reply.

He scowls at me. Matteo looks mad that I interrupted him, so I close my lips tighter.

"You should know, my brother wasn't half the man I am. I'm gonna take good care of you," he says, and his meaning is clear.

I back up as far as I can into the door.

But it's no use.

Matteo is fast for a small man.

He grabs my thigh with a bruising grip and pulls me towards him.

Next, he presses his hard mouth to mine and I feel his tongue lick the seam of my lips.

I don't open them.

I struggle against him. He grabs my arms, and it is too hard. He is hurting me.

"Stop, please," I beg, and it is the wrong thing to do.

He pulls my hair and licks the side of my face till his mouth is by my ear.

"Why should I stop, you little whore? You're mine now. You got no man. No father. No one to fight for you. I am all you have, and I'm willing to give you my name. That's it struggle. Run. Hide. I will always find you," he says, and it is like that turns him on.

Shock hits me like a slap to the face. Confusion, too. I stop struggling and look into his dead shark-like eyes.

"Your name? What are you talking about?" I ask as I lean away from his hold.

But Matteo does not let me move.

He just keeps coming. He's insistent. And he's strong.

I know he can overpower me, so I try to keep him talking.

I can feel his hardness against my side as he kneels and tries to kiss me again, and it is revolting.

"You were gonna marry my brother, I can take his place," he says.

"What? I wasn't going to marry him, Matteo. We barely knew each other."

"My father already agreed."

"I'm sorry, but your father doesn't tell me who I'm going to marry," I scoff, and shake my head.

"Ha! You don't know shit about life, *nena*. Enrico Sanchez makes the rules. And I am his son. I get what I want. Now hold still," he grunts, and grabs my face harshly.

Then he kisses me again and squeezes my breast painfully hard with his other hand.

Bile fills my throat.

I wonder if he's going to rape me, but thankfully, the SUV stops.

I look out the window to see we're at my house. I open the door and fall out to my knees. Tears stain my cheeks, and I wipe at them, not sure what is actually happening.

Is this real?

Matteo follows me, and I am aware we have an audience.

"Oops. Clumsy," he grunts and tries to help me

stand but I do it myself, avoiding eye contact with him.

I race up the stairs and instead of stopping to chat with those who came by to offer condolences.

I lock myself in my room.

That night, I talk to my mother.

There are bruises on my cheek, breast, and arms where he grabbed me, and I'm doing my best to cover them. But Mami sees them, and she cries.

"No, no, no, *mija*. We have to get you out of here."

She is right. Much as it pains me.

It takes hours to come up with a plan, but we have one.

Even if it sucks.

Mami is still in shock, but she is levelheaded about this. About getting me to safety. And I love her for it.

"Maybe he'll leave me alone," I try to come up with an excuse to stay.

But we both know he won't.

"No, *mija*. I know all about Matteo. Your father told me. He is cruel and depraved. He is not a good person. I don't want him around you, Mia."

"I don't want to go," I whisper, and we are both crying now.

"I know. It will be okay. Papi would not want you

to stay here with that man after you. I've heard about Matteo. He does not have a good reputation with women. I know you are innocent, *mija*. Matteo would break you."

She hugs me tight, and I am sobbing. I feel like a small child. I just want to curl up on her lap and have her make the hurt go away.

But that's not fair. My mother can't go up against Enrico Sanchez's son.

The only way is for me to go.

"I'm scared. What if I leave and he does something to you?"

"Nothing will happen to me, Mia. Sanchez promised me I would always be protected," she offers me a sad smile.

"But what about, Papi? Will we ever know what really happened to him?"

"Sweetheart, your father was killed by the same men who killed Carmine. His death won't go unanswered. Meanwhile, you go. Live your life free from all this."

"I don't want to leave you," I cry, leaving the fat, soggy tears where they fall.

"You're not leaving forever. You'll come back, and we will stay in touch."

It breaks my heart, but she's right.

So, that night before I leave, I set up a dozen aliases and fake social media accounts and show my mother each and every one of them.

I might be abandoning her, but I need a way to contact her.

The tears don't stop as I pack a bag, and they fall even harder when she hands me a duffel bag stuffed with cash.

"How much is this?"

"Sixty thousand dollars and a new identity. Papi always had papers for us all, just in case. Maria Mendoza. That's your name now. You finish school wherever you land, and you keep me updated. I love you, *mija*," she says, clutching me tight.

I thought she was falling apart before, but I should have known better.

Like most women, my mother is stronger than others give her credit for.

She's a goddamn warrior, and I hope like hell I inherit half her strength and grit.

"I'll be back, Mami. It's not forever."

"I know, now go. Be safe," she says and kisses my forehead.

It's so damn hard, but I turn my back and I leave the only home I have ever known.

CHAPTER ONE-LUC

Being a fool for a woman was my father's downfall. When I was barely ten he left my mother for a waitress at his favorite dive bar.

He just left one day. Packed a suitcase and walked out the door, leaving me alone with no male role model and my sister to die in an alley from her drug addiction seven years later.

I tracked him down right after she OD'd. Fucker was slumped over the barstool, a shadow of himself.

The waitress took him for a ride. Emptied his bank account. Left him broken and pathetic.

I remember how I felt looking at the small man he became. Shriveled up and used.

He cried and asked me for money. I shoved his filthy hands off me and spat at his feet.

Anger.

So much fucking anger.

But I made a vow right then. I would never be a fool for a woman.

But here I stand. In my office, like the viper I am creeping around the shadows, lying in wait.

My dick is so fucking hard as I watch the security monitor. Of course, that's because I'm looking at the front bar.

At her.

There's just something about Maria Mendoza that strikes me as false.

Like she's hiding something behind her carefully straightened dark hair.

Even that doesn't seem right.

Not that she looks bad or anything.

Quite the contrary.

The woman is hot as fuck. She's been working for us for the past seven months, and in that time, I've done nothing but watch her.

I've watched her work. I've watched her flirt to get better tips. I've watched her in her silent moments when she thinks no one is looking.

And I've watched her watching Nico. He's the king of the Vipers. My boss. And my best fucking friend.

Her interest in him is what's stopped me from approaching her.

There are certain lines guys like me don't cross. Fucking with another man's woman is one of them.

But is she his woman? Was she ever?

Nico has a wife now. A pregnant wife.

For all intents and purposes, the king has found his queen, and it isn't Maria.

I've been watching to see how she handles it.

Coiled in my den. Eyes glued to the monitor. I wait patiently like the snake I am.

I'm pretty good at reading people, and Maria's reactions to this situation are puzzling.

She doesn't behave like a jilted lover or jealous girlfriend. I'm not in the habit of asking the king who he's fucking, even if the idea of him touching her makes me want to commit homicide.

Still, her response to his obsession with his wife is, well, *it's good.*

I am pretty sure they never fucked, which means I don't have to fight with my blood brother. Because I would. For her, I definitely would.

And that's bad.

I'm thirty-eight years old, got my law degree from Princeton. I even passed the BAR exam.

But I don't work for a law firm. I don't need to. I have one client.

Viper Enterprises.

My expertise is corporate law. I know criminal law is what most people expect, and while I have experience and knowledge there, it isn't my specialty.

And you see, that's what makes people so fucking predictable.

I don't need to know how to defend the Vipers. We have another guy who does that should the odd criminal charge be filed against one of us.

No, what I need to know is how to win against the elite. The guys in Forbes magazine. The corrupt politicians skimming from their own campaigns and taking handouts under the guise of being lobbied.

They're the real bad guys. The politicians. The lobbyists. Both of them.

Corporations are the biggest fucking criminals, and New Jersey is ripe with them.

Developers from out of town and overseas are always coming in and trying to muscle locals out of their land and businesses, making it hard for people to simply live.

The Vipers don't like that. In fact, we fucking hate it.

New Jersey is full of people who immigrated to this country with hopes for a better life. We've even got a big fucking statue sitting right in the Hudson River. That great lady constantly holding her torch, symbolizing freedom, never wavering.

I believe in that lady. And I believe in giving the little guys a chance. So fuck anyone who tries to come here and muscle us out under the guise of beautifying the state or whatever the fuck.

With Viper Enterprises buying up land and taking over mortgages, we have the power to turn those assholes out on their ear.

And it's everything I've ever wanted. Power. Influence. The ability to right wrongs.

No different really than kicking some fucking peddler off a street corner I've already claimed.

There are *drugs*, then there are *drugs*.

Money.

Power.

Control.

Those can be drugs, too.

On paper, I'm the lawyer representing our legitimate business. Yeah, I wear a suit and tie and everything.

Custom fucking tailored.

Behind the scenes, though, that's where my true

colors really shine. Because that is where I'm Council.

My job is to know every fucking thing there is to know about a situation and to report back to the man himself.

There can be only one king. One head to control the Vipers.

Nico Fury is our king and he has my unwavering loyalty.

The bond I have with him, and with Angel, his cousin, our Enforcer, is unbreakable.

Forged on the streets when we were young, hungry, and maybe a little stupid.

There isn't a damn thing in the whole fucking world I wouldn't do for my two blood brothers.

So, when Nico told me to get my law degree, I did. He's not college educated, but he's the most cunning motherfucker I ever met.

Over the years, we've established the Vipers as the most feared fucking organization on the East Coast.

And now that we're pushing legit, well, it's only gotten more interesting.

Every meeting with businessmen, politicians, and society assholes is like a chess match. But I'm good at playing chess, so I am always prepared.

It's all about anticipating your opponent's next move.

Life is like that, too.

Take my obsession with Maria, for example.

I've watched her watching Nico, and I've watched him ignore her. I've witnessed her reaction to Anna from day one. That's Nico's woman.

Naturally, I wait for Maria's next play. Beautiful woman like her, she's got to have a move or two.

But as the weeks pass, she doesn't vamp him like I expect her to. In fact, she's rather graceful about his rejection.

Interesting.

Myself? I don't take rejection well. Maybe it's because of abandonment issues from my father leaving.

I don't know. I'm not a psychiatrist.

I am sure there's a whole slew of shit therapists would have a field day with if I ever went for counseling.

But I won't. I can't. All my mess is what makes me the perfect man for this job.

Anyway, it's probably why I have yet to approach her. My aversion to rejection.

But still, I watch her. I can't seem to make myself stop. She's an enigma.

A mystery.

And she's piqued my curiosity.

It's not even late yet and I have a shit ton of work to do in my office, but I'm at the Vipers' Den instead.

Something about Maria won't allow me to do anything else.

It's like I'm waiting for something. For some signal or sign from the universe that will rouse the viper in my soul from his dark cave, wake him from his slumber.

I watch Anna walk in, her round belly showing in the little dress she has on. She's with her best friend Giselle, the same woman who a few weeks ago tossed a full pint of beer into my man Angel's face.

They sit in the king's booth, and I grin. It still awes me that Nico has a wife and a baby on the way. I never figured him for a family man, but I guess I was wrong.

It makes me wonder.

It makes me hope.

I clear my throat and adjust the cameras back to the object of my obsession.

Maria looks thoughtful. She isn't smiling, and that's unlike her. I want to ask her what's wrong, offer to help.

But that's not something I should do.

From the beginning, her eyes have been on Nico, and now that he's decidedly unavailable, it's the perfect time, really.

But do I want to be someone's second choice?

I grit my teeth. No, of course I don't. But I want to be Maria's choice.

The number doesn't matter.

Shit.

I've always considered myself a patient man, but when I see a half drunk motherfucker step to Maria while she's tending bar.

Well, I kind of lose my shit.

CHAPTER TWO-MARIA

I make a mental note to buy more color depositing conditioner. Sometimes it's shampoo. But I think the conditioner works better.

"Shit."

I hiss and check the phone. I'm late and I don't have time to order it now. I sigh, aggravated for no good reason.

I know coming back to my home state means having to stay incognito. But it makes me angry. It's just one more thing I miss about my old life.

My natural hair color, I mean. It's dark brown, like chestnuts, and I have gold and reddish highlights. It's also wavy and long, hanging down to the middle of my back when loose.

But ever since I came back to New Jersey to be

closer to my mother, I've been straightening it and using the most natural hair coloring treatment I can find.

I don't want to dye it. Nothing so permanent as that.

I walk out of the shitty little basement apartment I'm renting, and I groan.

"Why is it so fucking hot?" I mutter and start fanning myself.

I work at the Vipers' Den. It's already six, and usually I am at the bar by now.

But I'm running late.

I went to five o'clock mass to see my mother at St. Aloysius' Church. It's the only time I get to see her.

We don't acknowledge each other in public. But today I sat two rows behind her, and I swear I smelled her perfume.

There were tears in her eyes as she walked past me when it was over. And I understand, I do. I cried, too.

I want to be able to hug her. To talk with her in public. To visit my childhood home.

It's just too dangerous.

Matteo still comes by every couple of months, pretending to be checking in on her and commiserating with her over how *faithless* I am.

The man is crazy. Completely fucking delusional.

We were never dating, and the whole jilted lover act is absurd.

But he's dangerous. More so than ever now because his father is dead and there is no one holding the leash.

He scares me.

But my mother is all I have. When she was diagnosed, I knew it was time, so I came back.

I try to see her at church every other week.

Mami is so thin and frail. My chest squeezes and I sniff.

Cancer is a motherfucker, but the doctors are hopeful.

I want to be able to visit her at home, accompany her to her chemotherapy and doctor appointments.

But I can't and it is killing me.

Part of the reason I sought the Vipers was to maybe catch the attention of their king and get his help with this delicate situation.

A desperate, stupid plan.

I'm embarrassed about it now.

But Nico has been kind to me. And he's chosen to let it go.

Thank goodness.

Even better, I kind of like his wife.

Maybe we can be friends.

I don't know if it's possible. But I want to try. I don't have many of those.

Loneliness is a bitter pill to swallow, and I feel so alone.

Maybe that's why I chose bartending as my profession. It gives me a chance to talk to people with the safety of having the bar between me and them.

It sounds weird but think about it.

Waitresses get harassed and groped. It sucks, but it happens.

But bartenders?

Nah.

We're courted and respected by our customers. It makes sense, right? If you harass me, you don't get your drink. Period.

Who wants that when they're at a bar looking to kick back with their friends, have a couple of drinks, and a good time in general?

It's the perfect job. Of course, there are certain people who get rough.

But that's what bouncers are for. And the Vipers' Den has the best.

You don't fuck with the people who work here.

It's one of the attractions.

I know all about the Vipers.

Heard whispers of them before I left six years ago. Sure, Papi and Mami kept me sheltered.

But I'm not stupid.

If anyone can take Matteo Sanchez on, it's the men running this organization.

But since I failed to catch Nico's eye, I don't see why they would.

So, I just have to suck it up and hope being an employee is good enough.

"Hey, you got any change?" an older man in tattered clothes asks from the stop he's sprawled out on.

I can smell the booze reeking off him from where I'm standing, but who am I to judge?

"Hey Harold, how are you?" I say and reach into my pocket for a couple of singles.

"Good, Miss Maria, thank you kindly," he replies and stuffs the bills in his pocket.

"Be safe, Harold."

"You know I will. You too, pretty lady."

"I'll bring you some takeout later," I tell him as I wave goodbye and jog to catch the bus.

By the time I arrive at the Den, my palms are sweaty, and I feel anxious. I don't know what it is.

I mean, nothing happened at church.

No one recognized me or seemed to notice me at all. I made eye contact with Mami once when I received communion, but that was it.

I tug on the bottom of the silk tank top I'm wearing and smooth my palms over my tight black pants. On my feet, I have my most comfortable pair of leather boots.

Yes, I'm wearing boots in the summertime, but they're practical for my job.

This is my usual attire for tending bar. There are no uniforms at the Vipers' Den and I'm glad.

Half a dozen silver bangles clink together as I walk to the front door and the sound soothes me. Almost like bells.

I'm wearing two pairs of silver dangling earrings that match, and every time they touch my shoulders, I get shivers down my spine.

Biting my lip, I head directly for the bar.

"You're late," Antonio, another bartender tells me unnecessarily.

"Sorry. I'll close tonight if you like," I reply.

It's my way of apologizing. Antonio nods. He's married with two kids, and I know he likes to get home as early as possible.

He's been working here longer than me, but I

have been given just as much responsibility as he has, if not more.

"You're a gem, Maria," he says, and I smile, but it's forced.

Maria is my middle name, and I feel like a liar using it without telling people that.

Like some underhanded, devious snake.

But it's the best I can do, so I just swallow the guilt and my unease along with it.

By seven, the crowd is shuffling in nicely, and I am hoping to bring in a lot of tips. Mami's newest medical bill just arrived, and it is a doozy.

I see Anna Fury and her friend, Giselle, sit down at the king's table and I head over there. Time for me to make amends.

I sort of had it in my idiot head to catch Nico's eye and maybe get him to have Matteo back off.

It's been six years since I left home.

Six years since his brother and my father got killed.

I can still remember how scared I was after Papi's funeral when Matteo got handsy with me in the back seat of his SUV.

Sometimes I feel like maybe I made too big a deal of it. Then I remember his cold eyes and the way he looked at me like I was a piece of meat, and I know I made the right decision.

Also, he keeps tabs on Mami. Knowing that makes me feel even more secure about leaving in the first place.

But I can't stay gone. My mother is sick and I'm not leaving her again.

Everything is just so fucked up.

But I'm glad Nico has Anna.

I don't think I could ever be with a man like him.

He has this wildness about him. Like he can't be tamed. Even more so now that he has Anna, and she is having his baby.

Nico is unhinged.

Scary.

Powerful.

His cousin, Angel, has the same powerful build, but he's even bigger. And he terrifies me.

Truth is, I've always been more attracted to the quiet types.

My mind immediately goes to Luc Batiste.

The Vipers' Council.

How one man can be a council I am not sure, but he is.

Maybe it's some multiple personality thing.

Or maybe it's because on top of being a criminal, the man is an ivy league graduate and a lawyer.

There are many sides to that one. I wouldn't mind getting a chance to explore them.

But I shove that thought away.

Luc isn't interested in me. Why would he be? He's tall and lean, like a rodeo cowboy. He has gorgeous curly hair and steel-colored eyes that make my knees weak.

Usually, he's dressed in all black. Tailored shirts and pants that fit his hard body like a second skin.

But once, I saw him without his shirt and holy fuck. The man has a sleeve of black ink up his left arm.

So sexy.

Just like him. Luc is so tall and wiry. He looks sleek and rough.

I know he's tattooed, and I wish I could ask him to take off his shirt so I could see them in detail.

But I can't do that. I wouldn't dream of it.

He has piercings in both ears and his left eyebrow. Metal bars, but I have no idea if they're steel, white gold, or what.

So fucking hot.

He catches me looking at him time and again but he doesn't tease or smirk.

He just stands there. Quietly. Then he walks away.

So, whatever I may think of how hot the man is, he's clearly not interested in me.

No.

Hiding behind a man won't save me.

I know eventually I'll need to face Matteo, and I'll need to tell him to back off. But that's a worry for another day.

Right now, I'm going to attempt to make friends with Anna Fury and hope she'll forgive me.

Fingers crossed.

CHAPTER THREE-MARIA

Anna and Giselle turn out to be really wonderful.

Sweet, pretty, kind.

I make them two Orange Crushes, sort of a Jersey specialty drink. One is virgin for the expectant mama, but the fresh orange juice and splash of lime soda are still delicious.

I can see by the way they act with each other, they've been friends for a long time.

My chest gets tight, and I wonder if I'll ever have something like that. Maybe I could have. I mean I had friends in high school and college. Maybe I still would, if I hadn't run away.

But I did run.

And that changes everything, doesn't it?

I know without a doubt I was an idiot coming to this place, searching for sanctuary.

I see the way Nico is with Anna, and I know now that I was just kidding myself, thinking I ever stood a chance.

He was never for me. Truth is, I don't feel that way about him.

I don't feel that way about anyone.

It is hard to catch feelings when you're always in costume. That's what this is.

My bartender ensemble. My name. Maria. It's all a costume, right?

I mean, that's how it started.

But I see Giselle and Anna with her man, and I wish for things I have no right wishing for.

Companionship.

Friendship.

Love.

If only there was a man for me. But he would have to be special, you know?

Like someone who won't mind that I've never even seen a dick up close and would have no idea what to do with one if I did.

Someone who won't care that I'm a bonafide liar.

I shake my head. Tired of the same old pity party.

Get a grip, I tell myself.

I'm not here to make friends or find love. I am here because Mami needs me.

Someone is shouting for a bartender, and I wave goodbye to Giselle and Anna and I turn to my next customer.

The bar is crowded, and the DJ is slamming tonight.

The Viper's Den is a total hot spot. So deceiving from the outside. But lies are a real theme around here.

The Vipers pretend to be regular businessmen, but I know the truth. They're criminals. Gangsters. Mafia. Whatever you call them, it all adds up to one thing.

They are violent, unhinged criminals.

And I am surprisingly okay with that. In fact, I need that in my life.

The Vipers are the only ones I know strong enough to take on Matteo Sanchez.

His brother Junior has taken over the cartel, and word is, he turns a blind eye to the nefarious goings on of his brother.

I cringe as I think about Matteo's threats, and the plans he has for me if he ever finds me.

It seems silly after six years, thinking he is still looking. But I know it's not silly.

He's been coming by more frequently, ever since Mami got sick.

That rotten bastard is crazy if he thinks I will ever be his.

"Yo! I'm trying to get a drink here," the customer shouts, and I snap my gaze back to him.

Terrific.

He's obviously drunk, even though it's early. I'm already shaking my head even as I place a glass of ice water down in front of him.

"Have some water," I say, but he glares at it.

"What's this? Nah, baby, lemme get a shot of Henny," he slurs.

I bite the inside of my cheek to stop from rolling my eyes.

I can't tell you how many people try to put on a front, pounding back shots of Hennessy like they are superstars, instead of savoring the cognac as is recommended by experts.

I'm not particularly fond of the stuff myself.

We just got a new shipment of platinum bottles from Whiskey Neat, and I have to admit I love that Jersey based label.

"Sorry, no can do. Have some water right now, okay? I can bring out some pretzels and check on you in a bit," I say, trying to placate him.

"Did I ask you for pretzels, *puta*?" he explodes.

He slaps the glass of water, so it shoots backwards and spills all over the bar and splashes on my face and chest, plastering my silk shirt to my skin.

He steps on the footrest and reaches over the bar, his hands clawing at me.

I don't know why I can't move or run or, I don't know, *something*.

But I can't.

I'm just frozen in place. Like a statue.

My heart is beating a mile a minute and I'm breathing like a marathon runner as flashes of another man's hands grabbing at me come flooding into my brain.

The bar is dark, but there are ambient lights. This man is just the right height and build to remind me of Matteo, so maybe that is why I can't move.

I flinch when he's about to make contact. Then, suddenly, he's lurching backwards. Like some invisible force has taken hold of him and is pulling him away.

I exhale.

Then I focus.

That force I mentioned. It is not invisible. I squint, peering past the stumbling man's image.

That's when I see *him*.

Luc Batiste.

Only, he doesn't look like the Luc I know.

His face is twisted in a feral sneer. His posture is stiff. Like his body is wound tight.

Coiled.

Like he's about to explode.

Then, I watch in total and complete shock as he does just that.

"Don't. Fucking. Touch. Her."

Each word is punctuated with a punch to the face.

Spoken between gritted teeth.

Luc growls, as he drags the man away from me.

"Get the fuck off me, man," the stranger says, trying to break free as blood flows from his nose.

But he can't.

Luc has him by the neck, like the stranger is some errant child.

His steel eyes flash to mine, then he turns, fast as a snake, and continues pummeling the holy hell out of the drunk man.

My eyes widen. I watch the unmitigated violence I had no idea Luc was capable of take over.

His features shift. His steel eyes glitter. He changes from the quiet, careful man I thought I knew to something else. To a predator.

A viper.

True, I've only spoken to Luc a handful of times since I came to the Vipers' Den, looking for work, and more.

I returned to New Jersey after six years, thinking if I could get someone powerful to take me under his protection, I would be safe.

I thought the king was that man.

But Nico isn't mine.

And I have yet to feel anything other than anxiety about being back in my home state.

Only, right now, as I stand there watching Luc beat the crap out of that drunk stranger, I think maybe I wasn't looking at the right man to begin with.

I was wrong about Nico. And it looks like I am wrong about Luc.

From what I've heard, Luc is this intellectual who abhors physical conflict.

He is a lawyer. A considerate man. Not a hothead, right?

He doesn't get his hands dirty. At least, that is what I thought.

Over the past few months, I thought I learned all about the hierarchy of the Vipers.

Angel is the muscle.

Nico is the king.

Luc is the brain.

But I was mistaken.

Luc is more than that.

Quiet.

Smart.

Classy.

Hot as fuck.

And violent. Very, very violent.

Also, way out of my league.

That last part is not debatable. He is out of my league.

I like smart guys. But I always knew I would need someone strong if Matteo was going to be a problem. His visits to my mother tell me he will be.

But maybe I've been going about it wrong. Maybe I don't need strong. Maybe I need smart.

Or maybe I need both. Someone smart and strong.

Like Luc.

But there are no other guys like Luc.

I watch, stunned, as he unleashes hell on the squat, drunk man.

Until Angel finally pulls him off.

His chest is heaving and his eyes glitter like the silver piercings in his ear and eyebrow.

The music is still blaring and there are a small team of bouncers surrounding the area, pushing nosy customers back.

Really, it is chaos.

But I don't care.

I don't pay attention to any of it.

I am too busy watching Luc.

The mask he usually wears in public is gone.

And I see the real Luc.

No, I don't know everything about him. But maybe it's time for me to learn more.

I lick my lips as he steps back once the man stops moving.

His face is still warped in an angry snarl, but I'm not scared of him.

I feel breathless and warm all over. And I'm eager for what he's about to say.

Luc turns to look at the man bleeding all over the floor and he spits.

Then he wipes his mouth with the back of his hand.

And he looks at me.

"My office. Now."

CHAPTER FOUR-LUC

I don't often give into my rage. Anger unbound is a destructive thing.

Weaponized, it is downright lethal.

That's how I feel when I see that asshole reach across the bar for Maria.

Lethal.

Fucking homicidal.

Physical violence is no stranger to me. But I prefer to exact my vengeance in other ways these days.

But every now and then, someone asks for it, and this motherfucker is asking for it.

The second I spotted him moving in aggressively towards Maria, I leave my office where I've been watching the security feed for the last twenty minutes.

Nodding at Anna and her friend as I pass, I frown as I move closer to the bar.

To her.

I don't know how I know shit is about to go bad. But I always know.

It's part of why I'm the fucking Council.

Violence is not the answer to everything. But it is the answer to some things.

I learned that very early in life.

Usually, I keep certain things locked up tight in compartmentalized boxes inside my brain.

It's like a filing system.

I am not saying I have a photographic memory, but it's close enough.

Right now, I'm using my almost eidetic brain to bring up what I know about fighting.

Things I learned on the streets and everything Angel taught me.

I pull it all to me as I stride angrily across the floor.

I am close now.

So close, I hear that motherfucker call Maria a *puta,* a whore, and I push my sleeves up.

I'm already going to knock his teeth out for that.

But when he slaps his hand drunkenly across the bar, knocking over the full glass of water and hitting her with it, I lose all semblance of control.

I feel our guys surround us as my fist makes contact with that piece of shit's jaw.

Angel is there, too.

I can hear him calling me off, but I don't fucking listen to him.

I don't know what Maria is to me. I have no claim. No reason to behave this way.

I don't give a fuck.

I've come a long way from that street rat I used to be. But deep down, at my core, I am still who I am.

Luc Batiste.

The last in my family to survive this fucking city.

Lawyer.

Criminal.

Man.

I've done bad things in my lifetime. Some under the guise of doing good.

Others, well, others just because I fucking can.

Who we are, what we are, the Vipers?

Well, that's all I know.

But watching Nico and Anna, I feel like maybe I can be more.

Maybe I can have more.

She might have come here looking for the king. But she's gonna leave here with me.

It all starts with claiming. And as I spill the blood of this unfortunate fuck across the Den's floor, that's what I'm doing.

I am well aware of the consequences of my actions. But I don't stop.

I can't.

And with every punch I land across this fuck's miserable face I feel anticipation rise in my bones.

The crowd's been pushed back. The music is still thumping. And my heart is pounding inside my chest.

My opponent, though he isn't much of one, goes limp, and I drop his sorry ass on the cold floor.

Then I spit on the ground beside his head.

My gaze meets Maria's wide-eyed one, and I address her directly for the first time since I stomped over there.

Her shirt is clinging to her big tits, the silk hopelessly ruined and showing her nipples blatantly to any motherfucker with eyes. She's got water dripping from her hair, down her face, and her mascara is smeared.

Last thing I notice, there are shards of glass everywhere.

That's it. I can't take it.

"My office. Now."

I'm shocked I can even form sentences. My chest is heaving. Even though I just finished bashing my fist into this asshole's face, I'm still amped up.

But the idea Maria is hurt, possibly by some stray shard of glass, that she's just standing there soaked and stunned has me ready to go another ten rounds.

I turn my back and start walking to my office. The sounds of men getting the fuck out of my way reached my ears, and I hear Angel barking orders.

But those aren't the sounds I want to hear.

I close my eyes. And finally, I hear it.

Her footsteps. Right behind me.

Fuck. Yes.

I've been watching Maria for months. I know just the sound her leather boots make when she walks across the barroom floor.

Stalking her from the shadows has become my guilty little secret.

My obsession.

My passion.

I'm always watching her. Always wanting her.

But I never act. Except for now.

Tonight, by walloping that dude, I claimed her in front of the whole fucking nest of Vipers.

Tonight, Maria is finally mine.

CHAPTER FIVE-MARIA

I follow Luc down the darkened hall to where his office lies. It's a winding sort of path to his door.

I've only been there once. To drop off employee paperwork I filled out when I applied.

I didn't even go inside, I just slid it beneath the door.

Something about him was just so intimidating.

And not because I think he'll hurt me, just because he feels so, *so big*.

I shiver as I wait for him to scan his hand on the biometric lock and I'm not sure if it's because of the water soaking my outfit, or if it's just the company.

I'm gonna go with the latter.

Luc's office is in a separate hall than Nico's and

Angel's. Still, we have to go down a flight of winding, narrow stairs, but I guess it makes sense.

Nico and his cousin are so big. Their presence I mean. But Luc has an understated elegance.

He's always so focused. Unassuming. But like he just proved, he is as scary as the rest of them.

Silent.

Deadly.

Fast.

The layout of the Vipers' Den is nothing like other bars or clubs I've worked at. From the outside, it's unassuming.

Just your average *hole in the wall bar* you expect to find in any city. Another of the many brick buildings lining the streets.

But inside, it really is a den.

There are hallways hidden in plain sight. Sort of like tunnels running through the entire building.

It's a multilevel space, though the upstairs is VIP, and belowground are the Vipers' quarters.

The real deal.

Not the wannabes.

We get plenty of those. The Vipers' Den is the kind of place that draws certain elements.

Dangerous elements.

Hot shots come in occasionally. People who want to rub elbows with the criminal underworld.

Those guys are just playing dress up, though. The Vipers are real. Every bit as tough as the Sanchez cartel. And the Den is the perfect example of their power.

What other not so lawful organization has their headquarters so publicly known?

And why shouldn't they? Who the fuck is going to take them on headfirst?

The Vipers are everywhere. They're reach is far.

I know because I researched them. It's why I came here with my heart full of secrets and my mouth full of lies.

They don't know who I am or what trouble is stalking me.

The Den is roughly masculine.

Edgy and raw.

The ceilings have been ripped open. Everything is steel, cement, glass.

The ambient lighting is trendy. The bar is backlit, and we change the color depending on whatever.

There's an energy inside the Den.

It's like danger meets sex appeal.

It's the same energy I feel when I'm around Luc.

Whatever plans I had when I first came there to

check out the king of the Vipers, they're all so far out of my head now.

Luc opens the door for me and ushers me inside his office. I go willingly.

His office holds richly masculine furniture. There's an enormous waterfall desk with an epoxy river running through it and my mouth drops open.

I'm constantly watching reels and videos online with people making these things, and I am fascinated by the whole process.

But I've never seen one like this. The wood is black.

It looks burned or charred. And the epoxy, well, it's not teal or blue glitter frozen within. It's silver and gold, and it is magnificent.

Like starlight swimming in a sea of black.

The entire thing is highly polished. It looks like magic.

I shiver again.

Even though it is dark inside his office, I can make out the silver and gold glittering swirls.

Only the glow from several monitors he has mounted to the wall on long metal arms lights the space. I've never seen a setup like that.

It looks like he can swing the monitors around

when he wants to view them and push them out of the way when he's done.

Anyway, the glow of the monitors is enough to make that treasure of a desk gleam and sparkle.

I move to touch it, but suddenly a bundle of white terrycloth is blocking the way.

"Here," Luc says, handing me a towel from a closet hidden behind a panel.

I gasp.

I didn't see or hear him move, that's how quiet and fast he is.

"Easy, Baby Girl. I'm not gonna hurt you," he says in a voice that's much softer than the one he used earlier.

I nod stupidly.

I know he's not gonna hurt me.

Wait.

Does he think I am afraid of him?

"Thanks, Luc," I say, forcing the words out.

I have so many questions. So many things I want to say.

But first, I want him to know I am not scared of him.

"You're bleeding," he says suddenly, frowning as he moves to hold the towel to my neck.

I suck in a breath. He's so close now.

So close and still so damn far.

I don't know what's wrong with me. I know I should be scared and upset over that whole mess inside, but instead, I'm shivering like a virgin inside a lothario's bedroom.

I am a virgin. But that's another story.

My one great flirtation ended with a dead man, his creepy brother, and me having to flee my home. So, no, I wasn't exactly in a rush to pop my cherry.

But standing here, this close to Luc, I'm wondering if my stance about that whole thing has changed.

"Shit, I see glass in the wound."

"Is it big?" I ask, blushing at my words.

"What?"

"The cut and the glass," I whisper.

"No. Do you trust me?" he asks.

I pause, watching him as he goes completely still.

Then I nod.

Yeah, I do trust him.

CHAPTER SIX-LUC

*H*oly *fucking hell.*

I could've killed that man with my bare hands for what he did. Luckily, Angel brought me back to reality when I heard his sharp voice growl my name.

Then I saw Maria covered in water and glass, and my attention was diverted.

Now, she's here in my office and I'm both elated and nervous as fuck.

Imagine that.

Me.

Nervous.

I lead her to the bathroom by her hand and motion her to sit on top of the closed toilet while I gather some first-aid supplies.

We had to pass the bedroom to get here, and the door was already open. I know she saw it, and I don't know what she's thinking.

I mean, I want her.

I plan on fucking her.

But I'm not going to just pounce on her like some animal.

I take a deep breath as I face her, and I take the towel from where she's holding it against her skin.

Fuck.

She smells so good. Like honey and lilacs.

It's a combination of fragrances I never smelled on a woman.

It whets my appetite.

Makes me want to lean in close and drag my nose along her clavicle, down to where her plump breasts are straining against her destroyed top.

"This is ruined," I murmur, and I look into her eyes as I take her straps in my hands.

She nods. Then she shivers.

"You're cold."

It's not a question, and I know what I'm about to do is uncomfortable, but I can't leave her sitting in that fucking tank top.

Just looking at it makes me mad all over again.

I slow my breathing. Forcing myself to calm

down even as I grab the front of her shirt and I tear it right off her body.

Maria gasps, her hands move in front of her chest.

But I've seen tits before, and she's wearing a bra. It's not like I'm a fucking pervert.

Even if hers are the best fucking pair I've ever seen.

I tug the ruined material off her, forcing her arms down. Next, I grab another towel off the rack and I hold it in front of her.

"T-thanks," she murmurs, and wraps it around herself.

I grunt.

I'm incapable of words.

Seeing her vulnerable, and having her here in my space, is a lot.

I've fantasized about this very thing for months. Well, not exactly.

Like, not the part where a drunk dick hurt her.

I grit my teeth and I grab the tweezers and the disinfectant from the first-aid kit.

"This will numb the area," I whisper and spray it over her skin.

She nods.

"Hold still, Baby Girl," I tell her.

Altogether, I extract six tiny shards of glass from her skin. I clean her wound and apply antibiotic ointment and a small bandage.

It shouldn't scar.

Anger fills me as I think of that prick who did this to her, and I clench my jaw. I hate that she's hurt.

"Um, thank you," she says, and she sounds uncomfortable.

Shit.

I know I'm not doing anything to make her less stressed by being so closed off.

I already tore her fucking shirt off and accosted her without so much as an explanation.

Amazing, isn't it?

I'm a fucking lawyer. Words shouldn't be so hard for me.

But here I am, kneeling in front of this slip of a girl, and I can't think of one goddamn thing to say.

"D-do you have a shirt I can borrow?" she whispers, and I want to slap myself in the forehead.

"Yeah. Of course," I mutter, and I exit the bathroom.

I grab one of my undershirts and frown. I'm tall, yeah, and my shoulders are wide, but I'm not as big as Nico or Angel.

My build is leaner, and all my button downs are tailored for me.

Maria, fuck, Maria is hot. She's gorgeous and curvy, completely mouthwatering.

Her skin is a golden tan color, and I don't know if it's from being outside or it's just natural.

I fucking love it.

I love how she looks.

Maria looks soft to the touch. And I am dying to do just that. But I won't. Not unless she asks me to. She's been through enough tonight.

Besides, the point I am trying to make is I doubt my button downs can contain her tits.

They're big. Like more than a handful big, and I have big hands and long fingers.

My dick thumps behind my fly as I imagine squeezing those big beauties.

I hear her moving around in the bathroom and when I turn, I find her looking in the mirror. She's frowning as she inspects the bandage, but I'm not paying attention to that.

She's lifted her long hair into a ponytail, and damn, she looks so pretty. And young.

Maybe too young for me.

I don't know her age. Well, I know what her license says, but for some reason I don't believe it.

She doesn't look thirty-one.

It seems everything I think I know about this woman leaves me with another question.

I'm curious. And aroused.

I walk to the bathroom, and she spins to face me.

Maria reaches for the shirt, but I shake my head once.

Then I proceed to dress her.

It's intimate.

I'm standing close. So close I can see her pulse jump wildly as I glance at the vein throbbing in her neck.

I lick my bottom lip. It's a natural response. I can't help it, but I see her eyes widen as she stares at the bottom half of my face.

"Lift your arms," I tell her, looking down as she complies with my command.

Her breath catches as I tug the soft cotton over her arms and head. I pull the towel she is still clutching to her body away from her, and she sucks in a sharp inhale.

"Fuck," I whisper.

Her bra is made of some sheer black fabric, and it does nothing to hide her big, puckered nipples from me.

I keep pulling the shirt down, but I can't resist her. My knuckles rub over those hardened nubs. Like dark cherries. And she utters a tiny mewling sound.

My cock is practically screaming at me to do something. So I do.

I cup my hand behind her neck and I pull her to me.

"W-what—"

But that's all I allow her to say. I fuse my lips to her and crush them beneath mine.

This kiss isn't soft.

It's not gentle.

It is full of pent up desire and emotion.

I've wanted this woman for months. I've watched her pine after my boss and blood brother. But I have her now, and she isn't going anywhere.

All the time she's worked here, I've watched her avoid men, refusing their blatant passes.

It's part of the job, I know. But I don't like it. I don't want anyone hitting on her, and after tonight I doubt I have to worry about that particular thing any longer.

I rarely get into fistfights. At least, I don't anymore.

But the entire bar, the Vipers, Angel, and Nico,

too, all saw what I did tonight. They saw it and they will know what it means.

Maria is mine now.

Once I have the shirt in place, I step back and take a deep breath. I tell my dick to be patient.

I slow the kiss, aware that she's clinging to me with her tiny hands clutching my shoulders.

Fuck. Her honey lilac scent is inside my nostrils, and I want it to stay there for fucking ever.

I want to get drunk on it. But I can't. Not until she understands.

Maria's life has just changed, and she doesn't even know it.

But I have to tell her.

"We need to talk."

CHAPTER SEVEN-MARIA

A week passed since the incident at the Den, and I'm no closer to understanding how everything changed so fast.

The Den's security guards offer me a wide berth, and it's bizarre. I've worked here for months, and I'm on a first name basis with everyone.

But no one will talk to me now.

And it makes me feel strange.

Luc hasn't touched me since that incredible lip lock in his office. But he did explain some things.

It seems Vipers have rules.

His beating the shit out of that drunk guy was a big deal. It means I'm his now.

But that's the thing.

I don't know exactly what being his means.

My heart stutters inside my chest as I put my purse in the safe behind the bar.

I bite my lip and flip my flat-ironed hair behind my shoulders.

It's supposed to rain tonight, and I shouldn't have bothered, but I am so used to donning this costume, it's simply routine.

"Hey Maria, got a request?" Randy, one of the local DJs we have on our Friday night rotation asks me.

This is his first night back in over a month, so I'm sure he hasn't heard about the whole incident.

"Something fun," I reply, and he winks at me.

He's cute and young, flashy with his brightly colored tank top and a backwards cap on his head.

A harmless flirt, really.

I don't think about Randy after that, I just sway to the beat as I prep behind the bar. Fridays at the Vipers' Den are always packed.

Good thing, too. I need the tips. I just sent Mami everything I had in the bank through Venmo, but I forgot my phone bill is coming up and I need cash for that, too.

Once I'm done slicing fresh citrus and filling up my condiment tray, I head to the bathroom.

"Yeah, Girl. Work it!" Randy says over his microphone, and I raise my hands to the roof and give a little shimmy.

I'm laughing as I head inside the ladies' room to freshen up my makeup and straighten my outfit.

Tonight, I am wearing a tight red corset top with high-waisted, wide-legged black pants with slits down the sides. I love how they look when I walk.

I'm a big girl, but the corset cinches my waist. It highlights my cleavage, not my stomach. And the pants hide my thick thighs and plump ass.

Whenever I need money, this is the top I wear to tend bar.

I know. I know.

But it's not a sex thing for me. I'm not trying to pick up men.

Truth is more women than men tip me extra when I'm wearing this.

It's like some kind of *sisterhood girl power rah-rah* type thing. Like they want to cheer me on for not caring that society thinks I'm too fat for this outfit.

Fuck society.

I don't have a problem with self-esteem. I mean, I know I'm pretty. But I am also real enough to know I'm overweight. What most of the world considers unattractive.

Whatever.

Of course, I have doubts and I can get self-conscious.

I'm human, after all.

So, what if I'm still a virgin at the ripe old age of twenty-seven?

And what if I can't pull off a real sexy look because of my untouched state?

I mean, I'm pretty.

Cute, even.

I know I'm definitely not a vamp or sex kitten. Not like a lot of the women who frequent this place.

Hell, I'd probably fall on my face if I ever tried to really flirt with a man.

But the way I see it, there's someone for everyone out there, right?

Maybe someday I will find *my special someone.*

Of course, that can only happen after I am off Matteo Sanchez's watchlist.

I wish I could figure out what the hell Luc meant when he said I belong to him.

I mean, is he serious? I expel a breath and look in the mirror.

This man has a hold on me, and we only kissed once. It isn't fair.

Damn it, Luc.

The man has been on my mind all week. I've had

the last two nights off, so I haven't seen him since Tuesday.

I've heard his name plenty though from Sisi and Anna. Sisi is Anna's nickname for her bestie Giselle, and I can't even begin to describe how thrilled I am that she asked me to use it.

Anna is a little intimidating to me. Not because she's mean or anything. But she is married to the king. And I shamelessly chased him up until they got together only recently.

I want to be her friend though, and I'm making strides. Anna is a little shy, and it's understandable. Her husband is a lot.

Giselle seems to accept me right away. She's so open and outgoing. We kind of bonded the night she came storming into the Den, looking to take a piece out of Nico's hide for knocking up her best friend.

Only. Well.

Giselle kind of mistook Angel for Nico and tossed a full pint of beer in his face.

Ever since then, she and Angel have been engaged in some kind of sexually tense warfare.

I don't know. It's not really my business and our friendship is too new for heart wrenching confessions.

But I hope it will be.

Pulling my tube of shimmery lip gloss from my pocket, I glide the roller over my lips.

I don't like heavy lipstick, even gloss, and I am blotting it with a tissue when the bathroom door slams open.

"What don't you get about you being mine?"

My eyes flash upwards and I see Luc's steel gaze boring into me.

He looks *hot*. But also mad.

Like so fucking mad.

He's wearing a light gray button down and charcoal colored pants. The shirt is open at the collar and with his hands on his hips, the material stretches over his chest and biceps, and I can make out the dark outline of his tattoos through the material.

I swallow.

Feelings I'm not used to flutter inside of me, starting at my stomach and growing through my chest, my throat, all the way to my fingertips.

"W-what are you talking about? You haven't even seen me in days!"

"You were flirting with the DJ," he accuses.

"What? I was not!"

"I won't fucking have it, Maria."

I turn to face him, my chest heaving with indignation.

This fucker.

"You know, you barge in here bristling like some damn tomcat whose fur has been rubbed the wrong way, but you haven't even talked to me in days!"

His eyebrows disappear into the dark curls covering his forehead, but I swear I see the corner of his mouth twitch.

"Did you just call me a tomcat?"

I huff.

"Is that all you heard?"

Crossing my arms, I shake my head. Embarrassment heats my cheeks, and I'm at a loss.

I just don't know what to do with this man who says I belong to him, but doesn't seem to want me.

He'll probably freak out when he finds out I won't know what to do with him even if he decides to take me to his bed.

Still, I want him to try. I'm even a little hurt he hasn't touched or kissed me since that night.

Shit.

That's probably something I should keep to myself.

It's not like I can be honest with Luc. I can't tell him the truth about my situation. It's too risky.

What if he chases me away?

The Vipers are powerful. And I bring a certain amount of trouble they likely won't want.

But I can't leave now that Mami is in the thick of her treatment.

I've managed to pay down her bills, but I know she'll need help around the house soon. I want to hire a part-time cleaning service, maybe a nurse if she needs one.

But I don't have the money.

Yet.

That's what I tell myself.

This little lack of funds is temporary. I'll get there.

Someday.

The money Papi left us is gone now. I spent the cash she gave me just to live and go to school. She spent hers on the house and on her treatment.

"Are you hearing me, Baby Girl?"

"What?"

"Maria, when I said you were mine, I told you what that meant. You belong to me now. You don't flirt with other men. You don't fucking smile at other men. You certainly don't dance for them."

"Oh my God. He asked me if I had any requests while I set up the bar, Luc. It's not like I was doing anything with him. He's a DJ. It's his job to hype up the crowd. That was just practice," I try to explain.

"Yeah, well, I already beat one man into a trip to the Emergency Room for overstepping where you're concerned, and I'll do it again. I'm a Viper, remember? And this is our fucking place."

"I know," I murmur, but I'm not paying attention.

My mind is wandering. Thoughts of how good his lips felt pressed against mine fill me.

I sway on my feet as he steps closer to me. Luc is much taller than I am, and he's thinner than Nico or Luc, but he isn't small.

His shoulders are wide. His body is tight with muscles.

His steel eyes glitter like silver when he's worked up, and fuck yes, he's worked up.

So am I.

Why am I attracted to men who wear violence around them like some goddamn shroud?

There must be something wrong with me.

Luc cups my cheek in his hand and dips his head.

"After close, I'm taking you home," he says, and I nod.

I'm a novice, but I don't care. I want him.

Luc seems to accept my response. He hums deep in his throat, then he presses his mouth to mine.

His kiss tilts my entire world on its axis.

When he lifts his head, I can't even remember my own name.

Mia.

No, Maria.

Fuck.

"Tonight," he says, then he turns and leaves me alone in the bathroom.

I look back at my reflection, and I don't even recognize myself.

Did I say I couldn't pull off a sexy look?

Well, I was wrong. Something about the way Luc kisses the hell out of me has my eyes lust-glazed and my lips are pink and swollen.

I don't even need lip gloss.

When I finally grab my big girl panties and leave the bathroom, Luc is nowhere to be seen.

And neither is Randy. I bite my lip.

"Hey Maria, what's up?" Stella, another of our DJs, walks in with her gear.

"Hey Stella, did something happen to Randy?" I ask.

She shrugs.

"Don't know. I just got a call to come in."

I nod and walk back behind the bar.

He didn't, right?

But I think he did. I think Luc sent Randy packing.

I know it's heavy-handed and wrong that he fired the DJ over nothing, really.

But I kind of like it. I like his show of possession.

And I have no idea what that says about me.

I wonder if he means it. If Luc like actually *likes* me, or if I'm just a piece of property to him.

With any luck, I'll find out later tonight.

CHAPTER EIGHT-LUC

Eight hours.

That's how long I've been in my office. Just watching.

My monitors are turned on to my very own custom private security feed. The software system we have is phenomenal.

Something Angel and I cooked up. It allows each of the three admins, me, Nico, and Angel, to create our own feeds. As in, I can pick whatever fucking cameras I want to monitor.

This one I call Baby Girl. After my little nickname for Maria.

I can watch every angle of the bar, catch every moment of her working her shift.

Usually, she's bouncy and happy. Tonight, she seems thoughtful.

Like something is weighing heavily on her mind.

I get it. I do.

I was pretty ominous when I said tonight.

But the truth is, I can't wait anymore. I need to have her.

All week fucking long I played this game of cat and mouse, which was why I nearly laughed when she called me a tomcat.

I'm no tomcat. I'm a motherfucking viper. And I think it's time I show her.

Some fucking customer calls out for her attention and it's another reason I'm stuck inside my office.

If I sit out there, this amped up, there is no telling what I will do.

I already let the world know she's mine when I beat the piss out of that guy and took her to my office.

But they don't know I haven't fully staked my claim.

That I haven't fucked her yet.

They don't know the snake is curled up inside his lair.

Waiting for the right moment to capture and strike.

I know it, though.

I know it and the anticipation is driving me mad.

"It's almost time, Baby Girl," I tell the monitor, brushing my fingertips over the one displaying her face.

Fuck.

She's so pretty.

I know it's foolish to think this, but there's an air of innocence about her. Something that tells me she's hiding more than I think.

I want to know her secrets. I want to break open the triple locked safe inside her chest that she's hiding them in.

Maria doesn't know I feel like this.

She can't possibly understand the depth of my fixation.

It's an all-consuming passion.

A sickness, some would call it. But fuck them.

They don't know my need, my desire, my life. She's the only thing that interests me anymore.

Aside from work, of course.

But a man needs more than work.

Nico has his. And I want mine.

I open the drawer inside my desk, picking up the

remnants of her tank top. I should have tossed out that discarded scrap of silk, but I couldn't bring myself to do it.

I lift it to my face and breathe it in.

Honey and lilacs.

My eyes roll back inside my head.

I know the door to my office is locked, and no one is coming in. Just like I know there are no cameras inside here.

Just like Nico's and Angel's offices.

This is my sacred space.

It's a symbol of our brotherhood and the complete trust we have in one another.

And it's the only reason why I do what I'm about to do.

I lean my chair back, my eyes on the screen as I slide my zipper down. The sound is loud in the quiet of my personal den.

But that's okay. My office is soundproof, too.

I free my cock from my pants and tug on it, feeling the titanium rods pierced through my shaft and the captive bead ring circling from my mush-roomed head.

I have piercings all over both ears. Two in my left eyebrow. One in my tongue, but I usually take that out.

It's my cock piercings that seem to get the most attention. I mean, they are designed for pleasure.

Mine and hers.

The final one is just at the beginning of my shaft. I have a curved titanium piercing barbell with balls on the ends of that one.

I didn't start getting pierced with the intention of enhancing my or my partner's sexual pleasure. But since it does, I use it to do just that. When I have a partner, that is.

Fact is, there hasn't been a woman in months.

Not since Maria walked through the door.

"Fuck," I hiss, squeezing my dick with one hand and pressing her ruined shirt to my face with the other.

My eyes flick to the monitor trained on her face and upper body. She's mixing a bunch of cocktails for a group of women.

One is wearing a banner across her chest that says *bride to be,* but I don't give a fuck about her.

No, my gaze shoots right back to Maria and her gorgeous tits as she leans over to hand out the drinks.

I stroke my dick faster. Jerking off in my office like a fucking teenager, but whatever.

I need to take the edge off before I take her home

with me, and sitting here, breathing in her scent while I get myself off, watching her in real time, well, it does the trick.

I groan as I start to cum. Hot jets of sticky liquid cover my shirt and my pants and I curse.

Fuck.

Good thing I have spare clothes in my office.

I lick my lips, looking at Maria one last time before I get up to change.

The audio is on low, and I can hear the DJ switching tracks. I grin wickedly, agreeing with the Black-Eyed Peas as I strip down.

Tonight really is going to be a very good night.

Woo. Hoo.

CHAPTER NINE-MARIA

utterflies?

B I try to calm down as I wipe the bar and load the last of the glasses in the big plastic tub for one of the bussers to bring to the kitchen to be run through the dishwasher.

My stomach is clenched so hard, I might actually have abs by the time the night's over.

Yeah. Right.

I snort at my idiotic joke and shake my head.

But seriously, do people really call this feeling of anxiety and nervous anticipation butterflies?

It doesn't feel soft and gentle. Like a swarm of pretty butterflies.

It feels like I have fighter jets going at it inside my gut.

Maybe I'm worrying for nothing. Maybe Luc was just messing around.

Then I hear his voice.

"Baby Girl, you ready?"

I turn, my eyes wide.

"Just let me get my bag," I whisper my reply.

Tell him, Maria. Tell him you're a fucking green as grass virgin and he'll run the other way.

I frown at my inner voice. It's self-preservation, right? It has to be.

But I don't want to listen. In fact, I am not going to.

I'm tired of being afraid.

Of living day to day just working with no social life to speak of.

Of looking over my shoulder.

Of not being able to be with my mother through the toughest time of her life after Papi's death.

I want to grab this thing for myself. For once in my life, I want to have a little control.

I want to be with someone.

Someone I choose.

I grab my bag and lock the safe, then I turn to face him.

I expect him to be on the phone or something. But he isn't. He isn't working or talking to anyone else.

Luc's focus is on me.

He's waiting patiently *for me.*

I really should run. I should tell him something about the real me. But I don't.

His steel eyes watch every step I take towards him as I round the bar. His gaze drops to where flashes of leg peek through the slits on my pants and I bite my lip.

He hums that same growling sound I've heard him make a time or two, and it sends spikes of anticipation sizzling through me.

My pussy aches and I feel wet down there.

"Baby Girl?" He says the nickname like it is a question when I falter my next step.

This is it, Maria. Last chance to run.

I straighten my shoulders and meet his hungry gaze.

"I'm ready," I lie.

CHAPTER TEN-LUC

I hold the passenger door of my matte black muscle car and watch Maria slide into the seat.

Fuck. Me.

She is so fucking gorgeous.

This woman is going to be the goddamn death of me.

"Wow. This is beautiful," she says, but she looks so stiff in her seat it takes me a minute to figure out what she's talking about.

"The car? Thanks," I murmur, shifting gears as we move into traffic.

"I thought you all had drivers."

"When I travel with the boss, we have a driver. But I prefer to be in control," I tell her.

I bite my lip, looking forward to being in charge of other things tonight.

"So, you went to law school, right?" she asks, surprising me.

I dip my chin.

"Why do you do this, then?"

"What do you mean?"

"Well, you're obviously smart and talented, I wonder why you don't do your own thing. Be your own boss," she says.

I pause. It's a good question. An interesting one. But I wasn't expecting it.

Maria mistakes my silence for anger, and she starts apologizing right away.

"Oh God, I'm sorry. I didn't mean to pry. It's none of my business. Shit. I shouldn't have asked you that. I am so sorry," she says, and she's wringing her hands on her lap.

I stop at a red light, and I turn to face her, covering her hands with one of mine.

"Baby Girl, you can ask me anything, okay? I just wasn't ready to answer the question," I explain, and like I want her to, she settles.

"No, you don't have to answer that. I need to mind my own business."

She huffs, looking at our entwined hands.

I don't miss the tremble that rolls through her. And fuck, it's like it goes straight to my dick.

"To answer your question," I say as the light turns green and I'm forced to use both hands to shift into gear, "Angel, Nico, and I are the original members of the Vipers. But a snake has got to have one head, or it will tear itself apart going in different directions. Nico is the right man for the job."

Now, it's her turn to be silent. I sneak a glance and I catch her expression.

It's contemplative.

Thoughtful.

Once again, this woman surprises me.

But right then, I have no idea how many more surprises she has in store for me.

CHAPTER ELEVEN-MARIA

My eyes widen as Luc pulls inside an underground garage.

I expected him to live in the same condominium complex where I visited Anna with Giselle earlier this week.

But he doesn't.

"Wait there."

I don't understand until I see him striding around the front of the car, holding his hand up to stop a man in black, *a parking attendant perhaps,* from touching the passenger door.

"I got it," he murmurs and pulls open my door.

Luc offers his hand and I pause just staring at his long fingers.

Holy. Shit.

Who knew a man's hands could be so erotic?

"You coming, Baby Girl?"

My gaze flicks up to his, and I know the second he sees the double entendre click inside my brain.

Luc smirks and licks his lips before it turns into a heated smile.

No, Luc, I'm not coming. Not yet. But with any luck I will be.

I nod and clear my throat, taking his hand as he helps me out of the car.

Those fighter jets are back, and I'm so busy concentrating on putting one foot in front of the other, I'm quiet the whole way across the garage, which I realize houses two more cars and that's it, to what looks like an elevator door.

"I never saw a building with a locked elevator," I remark as he uses his handprint to open the thing.

The doors open silently, and I step inside.

"There's another one that opens to the security room. But they can't access my main floor without my approval."

"Wait, this building is yours?" I ask, stunned.

He nods.

"How did you manage that?" I wonder.

"I own the building, Baby Girl. Bought it when it was an abandoned warehouse. Worked with an architect to redesign it. Then, I moved in."

He shrugs like it is no big deal. But it is.

This place is huge.

An entire warehouse.

It strikes me then just how much money Luc has.

I stumble over my feet as we exit, but he saves me with a firm grip on my elbow.

"Easy," he whispers, and he's so close I shiver.

"Come on."

He uses the same biometric security system, scanning his hand before another door unlocks.

The world he reveals behind it is masculine and rich.

Minimalist.

"How big is this place?"

"Pretty fucking big, Maria. You really want to talk about it?" he asks.

I nod, because yes, I do.

I want to know everything about him. I look around, my hungry eyes eating up every bit of information I can gather.

"Okay. Well, I bought this old warehouse. I renovated it. It's my sort of loft meets mini mansion, and it is right in the heart of Jersey City. An ideal place to live, truly."

"Ideal? How so?"

"It's close to work. Close to Nico and Angel. But nobody around here knows me, and I like the privacy," he continues.

"I never thought privacy was possible to find in the city," I say, trying for a joke, but it's lame.

"Anything is possible when you have money and power. I've got both," he says.

"I also have state-of-the-art security. Oh, and I'm kind of proud of the fact this whole building operates on the greenest electrical and plumbing systems available. I have solar panels on the roof, even a small wind turbine. I've also got a rooftop garden with a swimming pool and one-sided see-through glass covering it. My garden is hydroponic. I grow vegetables, fruits, and herbs. I have a guy come in once a month to make sure the system is running efficiently. I've got a courtyard out back and there are plants there, too. Come look," he says, and pulls me with him to the big window facing the back.

I love it. There is a huge wrought iron fence covered in ivy on both sides, blocking street level viewers from seeing in.

It's on the Hudson River, so I know this must cost a fortune. But for a moment, I allow myself to feel like I belong there. With him.

And it is wonderful.

"See that? It's a stone path cutting through the rose bushes and hydrangeas. It leads to the water. The gate has a biometric lock too, and I employ around the clock security. Nobody can get around this building from the back."

"Well, no, not with those twenty foot high fences," I murmur.

"They're fourteen feet high," he corrects me, but he's smiling.

"Do you like it?" he asks, and I sense he is feeling vulnerable.

I'm shocked, but also grateful for that glimpse of humanity.

I'm starting to think he's superhuman.

But I know he is every bit as real as me. We might be different, but Luc is still a man. Just like I am a woman.

"Like it?" I repeat, turning to him. "Luc, it is incredible. Thank you for sharing it with me."

"Good, I want you to like it. I want you to feel safe here."

"I do."

"and I want you to feel safe with me."

"I feel that, too," I whisper. And it is the truth.

Yes, I've gotten used to shitty apartments, but before that, when I lived at home, my childhood home was small, messy, and loud.

But it was full of love.

My heart contracts inside my chest, and a pain of longing hits me hard. I miss Papi. It's been six years since we lost him.

But it's worse than that.

Matteo Sanchez robbed me of my entire family, of my friends, my whole damn life on the day of my father's funeral.

I've been carrying the guilt of my decision to leave home for so long. Especially with my mother's cancer.

Coming back might be dangerous, but I have no choice. Matteo stole enough from me.

Someday soon, I will have to face my fears.

I will visit my mother in the open. Stealing glimpses of her at church isn't enough.

Someday, but not now.

Now, there is only one thing I want, and it's this man.

This quiet, mysterious, ridiculously gorgeous man.

"Want something to drink?" Luc asks.

I shake my head.

I don't want anything to drink. I want to be in control of something in my life.

And tonight, I think I can be.

CHAPTER TWELVE-LUC

*G*oddamn.

Maria is inside my home, facing me, her chest heaving inside that piece of fucking lingerie she's been wearing in public all night, and I wanna howl like a fucking beast, rip it off her body and burn it so she'll never wear it again.

I also want to keep it.

I want her to wear that for me and me alone with a sexy pair of red panties to match.

Guess I'm a man of many contradictions, but there is one thing I am absolutely sure of.

I want this woman.

I feel the snake coiled inside my soul unwind. He slithers free, testing the air, catching the need wafting off her in waves.

I shouldn't do this. I should let her go home.

She'd be better off without someone like me.

My life is fucked up.

The Vipers mean everything to me. I spend all my time working to keep us safe, to keep us solvent and whole.

But Nico has a wife now. A baby. Why can't I have that, too?

I feel so fucking stupid. So needy when I have those thoughts.

But I have to admit they've been coming to me with increasing urgency.

Still, I won't force Maria. I'll find some work-around for claiming her like I did so publicly. If she wants to go, that is.

The question is, does she?

But when I open my lips, that isn't what I ask.

"Want something to drink?" I say instead.

Maria shakes her head.

Then before I can offer her an out, tell her I'll take her home, Maria slides her hands up my chest and around my neck, pulling me to her.

"Luc?"

She mewls my name. A question in her tone. But her voice is like sweet fucking music in my ears.

I groan and suck on her tongue, my hands

searching for the fastenings on that goddamn fucking corset.

I'm impatient.

Greedy.

Half out of my mind with lust. So, no, I don't take my time. I just find the general area, and I grab the material in both fists.

Then I tear.

Maria yelps, but I'm still kissing her, so I swallow the sound.

She pushes against my chest, and I lift my head.

"You ripped my top!"

I nod, licking my lower lip as I pull the thing off her body and bare her gorgeous fucking tits.

She tries to cover them, but I hold her arms down.

I can see from her expression she's more shocked than scared. That's good.

I don't want her scared.

And her nipples, *those big, glorious cherries*, are already hard for me.

"Fuck, Baby Girl, look at you," I murmur. "So fucking pretty."

I press both my palms against her tits, and I squeeze, shoving them up so I can lick across the tops.

Maria's hands find purchase in my hair as I lick and suck and bite on her sweet tits.

"Oh my God," she moans.

I bite down harder. Leaving a mark. And when I lift my head to see it, my dick is like fucking steel.

"The pants. Take them off," I command.

I am holding on by a thread and Maria's almost shy display is wreaking havoc on me.

It's like she's innocent. Or pretending to be. And I don't know what to do with innocence. I've never had it before.

Hell. I've been fucking girls since I was thirteen years old.

But it's been a while now, and I'm not used to being gentle.

She's staring at me with her big almond shaped eyes open wide like a doe, and fuck, I love that look. That expression.

It makes my cock pulse.

"I said, take your pants off, Baby Girl."

"Here?"

"That's right. Right here. I'm the only one who lives here. The only one who will see you."

"B-but the lights on, and the window—"

"Are you questioning me?" I ask, cocking my head as I undo the buttons of my shirt.

Her eyes glaze over when I pull it off, and I like that she likes what she sees.

I'm not one of those beefed up muscle heads, but I'm lean, and I know I look good.

I've got enough muscle, and it is not from some gym. My arms and pecs, and my six-pack are all hard earned.

I'm not a pencil pusher despite being a lawyer.

Women tend to like my body. Especially that V leading to my cock.

I never cared one way or another what anyone thought about my looks, but I care what she thinks.

And that fucks with my head.

I want to know what's going on inside her mind, but when I look, Maria's eyes are on my sleeve of tattoos.

Then I wonder what she'll think when she sees my pierced dick.

"Maria, you're not listening."

"What?" She seems dazed, standing there with her big tits out, just staring at me as I unbuckle my pants.

She's pensive. Her mind is racing, and she blurts out something that makes me want to grin. But I don't.

"You're acting like you own me."

It's a challenge, and I accept it.

"What you don't seem to understand, Little Girl, is I do own you. You belong to me now. You do what I say. And I say, get naked."

CHAPTER THIRTEEN-MARIA

Holy *fucking shit.*

Luc is like seriously hot.

He's taller than he seems. Over six feet. And to me, that's gargantuan.

He's ordering me around like I belong to him. Like he owns me.

"You're acting like you own me."

Shit. I don't mean to say that out loud, but I do.

I think he'll get mad, but Luc's lip twitches again like he might bust out laughing. Only, he doesn't.

He answers me, and even though I know it's twisted, that I'm fucked up, my panties get drenched at his words.

"What you don't seem to understand, Little Girl,

is I do own you. You belong to me now. You do what I say. And I say, get naked."

I swallow, eyes wide. But I listen. I take off my boots.

"Good Girl," he praises me and I fucking love it.

"I already told you when I got that creep away from you at the bar, and you came to my office, you're mine. I claimed you then. And I'm gonna claim you now. With my dick," he growls that last part.

I push down my pants, dragging my panties down with them. I'm aware that this isn't normal.

Not the situation.

Not the fierce attraction I feel.

Not the way my pussy is clenching on air, desperate for him.

But I don't care. Six years is long enough for me to wait to start living my life.

"Fuck, Baby Girl. You're a goddamn knockout," he says, and pushes his boxers off.

I look down, helpless to do otherwise, and my mouth goes dry.

Luc is hard. And big.

So fucking big.

And more. He's got a snake tattoo running across his hip and lower abdomen. Well, it's more like the snake's body. The neck of the beast sort of stops right at the top of his dick, leaving the actual thing to be the head.

And what a fucking head.

Luc's cock is enormous, thick, and long, and it's fucking pierced.

The barbells and jewelry sort of resemble the head of a snake. The silver balls strategically place to look like eyes, mimicking the markings all across the tattoo.

It's sexy as fuck.

Powerful.

Menacing.

Mine.

That's a dangerous thought, but I can't help it.

Suddenly, I am very jealous of anyone else who might have seen him this way.

"Get over here, Little Girl," he commands, and his voice is so gritty and rough.

I like it.

I like it a lot.

I bite my lip. My pussy clenches again.

Moisture is dripping down my thighs, but I walk to him.

I'm completely naked and I know I should feel embarrassed, but I don't.

I'm jiggly and soft. My stomach is not like his.

He's all curved muscle and power.

My look is more like *she should have skipped dessert.*

But I don't.

And I won't.

I like food. I won't apologize for it. Some people are just chubby.

Nerves threaten to take over, and my second step falters. It's not the fancy rug he has covering the polished wood floors.

It's me.

I should probably tell him I've never done this, but I don't.

Because if I do, I worry he might stop.

And I don't want him to stop.

I might not be as pretty as him to look at. But I'm cuddly. And I want him.

I lift my gaze, and I look at him. I suck in a breath because no one has ever looked at me like that.

With abject hunger.

Such blatant need.

My pulse doubles.

Luc's eyes on me are like molten silver.

I know he likes what he sees, and it emboldens me. I straighten my shoulders and I keep going.

"That's it. Closer. Open your mouth. Kiss me, Baby Girl, and don't fucking stop until I say so," he says, ordering me around again.

I obey.

It's something I can't explain, but I want to listen to him. I need to.

I press my naked flesh up against Luc's body and I tilt my head, giving him access to my mouth.

But Luc doesn't just jump at me like I think he will.

His breaths are rough. Deep. But he's still as a statue.

Then I remember.

He told me to kiss him.

So, I snake my arms around his neck, and I pull him to me.

Next, I kiss him.

And I feel it down to my very soul.

CHAPTER FOURTEEN-LUC

I need Maria like I need my next breath.

I've been patient. Taking it slow.

Sure, she doesn't know I've stalked her for the past seven months. But I know it. My dick knows it. And I'm done waiting.

I drive my tongue into her mouth, sipping on her honey lilac flavor, and I groan.

My hands snake down her body, memorizing her curves, and grabbing her plump cheeks.

I pick her up, and she wraps her legs around me. I hold her with one hand on her ass and the other on her neck, keeping her kissing me as I walk us to the bedroom.

She's so fucking hot. I love the feel of her weight.

Maria isn't some waif, half-starved model wannabe. And I am so fucking glad.

I've had plenty of encounters with vapid women who were more concerned with my wallet than they were with me.

Those were one time deals. And I don't feel fucking bad about it. They used me, just like I used them.

But this is different.

Maria is not like that.

She's real.

Behind her secrets and lies, she's genuine.

But I don't like mysteries, and I plan to find out whatever it is she's hiding.

I want to learn every inch of her gorgeous self, inside and out.

Her soft body is the perfect foil for my hard one.

And tonight, I finally have her.

Three more steps and we're in my bedroom. It's simple, masculine.

Everything is made up in the same silver, gold, and black color palette.

What can I say?

I like the classics.

I drop her on the mattress, and she gasps. She's breathing heavy.

But so am I.

It's the first time I allowed either of us to come up for air since we started kissing.

She's sitting up, and I am kneeling on the bed. I can tell she's nervous.

But I won't give her room to get up. I'm not that fucking stupid. She's not getting the chance to get away from me tonight.

Maria looks a little like a scared rabbit about to flee. But in the wild, snakes eat rabbits all the time. And I mean to eat mine.

I lean over her, forcing her to lie back. She swallows, and I follow the movement with my eyes.

Fuck.

She's so good like this. All whimpers and moans.

The feel of her soft, heated skin as I slid my body over hers and position my thick dick at her entrance.

I want her on my tongue, but I need this first.

It's been months, and I need to stake my claim. Besides, there is always later.

"Are you on the pill?" I ask.

"What?" she blinks at me.

"Birth control," I reiterate, knowing I should have a condom on, but I can't bear the thought of anything separating us.

I want my stake to run deep inside this woman.

She's mine.

"I have an implant. It's good for another year," she whispers.

"Good."

Then I push forward. I don't wait I just flex my hips, my pulse is hammering, my heart pounding, and thunder is roaring inside my ears.

Months of waiting, of stalking from the shadows, and I have her now and she's mine.

Sure, the way we came together might seem abrupt to her or underhanded even, but I felt her kissing me inside. Just like I've felt her eyes on me whenever she thought I wasn't looking.

Months and months of this dangerous foreplay between us. And now it's come to fruition.

I expected her to drop the innocent act when I shove my cock balls deep inside her tight, wet heat. But she's not. In fact, she's squirming, and a sob wracks her body as I push through something I am sure as fuck not expecting.

"Maria? Fuck, Maria, you're a virgin?" I grunt the question.

Her pussy has me in a vise grip and I'm shocked and confused, but the caveman inside me wants to pound his chest and roar that my dick is the first one to ever be inside her.

The only one.

"Please, Luc," she begs me, wincing.

"I got you, Baby Girl. Relax for me," I tell her, and *godfuckingdamn,* my heart is drowning in a tenderness I didn't think I was capable of.

She clutches at my shoulders with her hands, her eyes squeezed tight.

I smile and it's an expression of such joy I swear I could pass out from it.

I cup her face with my hand.

"Look at me, Maria. That's it. Now, open your legs, drop those knees, and relax for me. I'm not gonna hurt you anymore," I tell her, and I mean it.

Once those big, almond eyes open for me, I stare into the glossy velvet depths, and I move.

Slow at first, gentle.

I stretch her channel, pumping my pierced dick, feeling every barbell roll and massage her inner core.

I dip my head and kiss her mouth, and I don't let up.

Maria moans and moisture pools between us.

She likes to kiss. And I fucking love kissing her.

Win win.

I start to move harder now, faster. Shoving my tongue into her mouth in time with my dick.

Maria moans. Her nails are digging into my sides

and my back. But she's not pushing me, she's pulling me tighter against her.

I'm seconds from blowing. Moments from coming inside this sweet virgin pussy. But I need her with me, so I lift my head and I meet her glossy-eyed stare.

"You're mine now, Baby Girl. Tell me."

"Yours, Luc," she whimpers and nods.

"Good Girl. Now, tell me what you want. You want to come?"

Maria is panting. Her big tits are squished between us, and she moans, nodding her head.

"Words, Maria. Tell me the words."

"I want to come, Luc. Please make me come."

I squeeze my eyes tight for a moment, then I open them and find her staring at me.

I adjust the angle of her hips, and I rear up, kneeling between her long legs and her juicy, thick thighs.

She's staring at me.

And I am staring at her.

That gorgeous body is jiggling with every move, and I love it.

Her tits bounce. Her rounded stomach is so soft and I'm running my hands over her skin, up to her throat.

I wrap my hand around it. I hold her there as I pump into her.

Then I take her hand, and I put it on her clit. Forcing her to touch herself, to rub herself in small, tight circles.

"That's it, Baby Girl. Touch that little clit. Rub it for me and come on this cock so I can fill you."

Maria's eyes widen.

Looking down, I watch my dick stroke in and out of her. I see the red stain there and I lose it.

Fuck.

I lose it.

"Luc!"

She is begging me.

Whether to ease up or to let her come already, I'm not sure. But there is only one way tonight ends. And that is with Maria's slick juices running down my junk.

I start to come.

Then I feel her arch her back and that already tight cunt of hers is squeezing and squeezing me as her orgasm rolls over her.

And it is mine.

She is mine.

This is mine.

And it is everything I ever wanted.

CHAPTER FIFTEEN-MARIA

A myriad of thoughts and moments stolen from time run through my mind as my body tries to come down from the high of having sex with Luc Batiste.

Holy fucking shit.

I had sex. Actual. Real. Hot as fuck sex. With Luc.

If what we just shared could even be categorized as just sex. But whatever.

I don't know what this means or where I stand with him. But I finally got to choose.

And I feel so fucking good. Luc's chest heaves and I watch him watching me as he withdraws his magnificent cock from my body.

It's hard to reconcile the man I think I know with this one.

Luc the Viper Council is usually so quiet. He even seems sweet sometimes.

But not in here.

In here he is different.

He's confident and merciless and I fucking love it. Devious might be a better word for him.

Like he wears this mask for the world, but here is where he reveals his innermost self.

And I'm honored he chose me to see it. Honored, he took me to his bed.

He keeps repeating that I'm his, but I don't know what that means.

All I know is I choose him right back.

My heart swells with emotion, and fuck, I think I might cry.

"Did I hurt you?" he asks, and he seems really concerned.

I shake my head.

He nods, like he understands.

Maybe he does.

I think maybe he knows what a big deal this is for a girl, a woman. Luc stands up and takes me with him, carrying me princess-style to the enormous bathroom I'm guessing is his.

The countertops are black marble with gold and silver swirls, and I inhale. It's like the rest of the place.

Opulent but tasteful.

No mess.

Nothing extra.

I'm messy.

I have three acrylic stands with face washes, creams, makeup, and other womanly potions in my tiny bathroom.

I shake my head.

He's so wealthy. And I know he is older than me. I don't fit in here. And the realization makes me sad.

"Stand up," he orders, and I look up to see he's standing in front of an enormous glass shower with six heads coming from the walls and one enormous rainfall showerhead coming from the ceiling.

It's amazing.

He turns the water on, waiting till the temperature is right. Then he leads me inside.

I glance down, and embarrassment fills me. There is blood painted against his cock, clinging to his piercings, and I bite my lip.

"What is it?" he asks, brows furrowed.

"I'm sorry," I sputter.

"Sorry for what?"

"About that," I whisper and dip my chin.

I am not sure how to deal with this and yeah, I'm like seconds from panicking.

"Maria," he says.

Luc touches a finger to my chin and lifting my eyes to his as water sluices over his shoulders and down his perfect abs.

"Don't be sorry for this. It's the biggest honor of my whole fucking life being the first man inside of you, understand?"

Tears roll down my cheeks, but I don't make a sound.

"Come here, Baby Girl. Let me take care of you. Let me clean you up and tuck you in, and we can talk more tomorrow. Okay?" he tells me.

I nod my head and he does just as he says. I'm beginning to think he always follows through.

He takes a soft fluffy loofah off a hook, and he pours body wash on it.

It smells like him. Something masculine and spicy.

Then, as I stand in his shower like a deer in head-lights, Luc starts to wash me.

"Turn around," he murmurs, and somehow this feels more intimate than when he fucked me only minutes ago.

The tears keep coming, but my crying is silent.

Luc just continues to watch as he runs the loofah then his hands up and down my body, over my breasts, and belly, my ass, and my sore pussy.

He turns the knob on one of the showerheads and cups some of the water. Then he cups my pussy with that same hand, and I yelp.

"Cold," I whisper.

"It'll help," he says, and I have to admit, he has a point.

He does it several more times. Just cupping the cold water and holding it where I still ache.

He washes my hair, and I almost don't remember the color shampoo I use, but his discerning eyes take it in as he watches the dark mess go down the drain.

My original color is lighter, with gold and red highlights. And as he conditions it next, I know he is curious about the waves and curls starting to spring back to life.

I feel overwhelmed with warring emotions.

Grateful.

Sated.

Needy.

Scared.

But most of all, I feel this glimmer of hope and with every passing moment it gets stronger and brighter. I'm not sure I should trust it, or him, but I can't help it.

This man is a conundrum.

Why did he take me to his bed?

Why does he say I'm his?

I want to be, I realize, and it scares the shit out of me. I want to belong to Luc. But he can have anyone. Knowing that, why would he want me?

He does. Obviously. I'm sure I wouldn't be here if he didn't. Luc kisses my head, and I swear I sway on my feet.

He is tender, but he can be rough. He's smart, but not a showoff. He's strong, I saw him kick that guy's ass.

He makes no sense. I can't fit him into any one square.

Maybe that's what I like about him the most.

Or maybe it's his pierced cock, my dirty inner voice says.

But I'm leery and nervous. Once he finds out I'm a liar, what then?

"I got you," Luc says, bringing me out of the downward spiral I'm headed in.

Before I know it, he has me wrapped in a towel.

He says he has me, but can that be true?

Does he mean it?

I expected annoyance or anger when he found out I was a virgin.

Maybe even scorn.

But Luc looks like I gave him a present, and to be honest, I gave him more than my virginity.

He just doesn't know it.

And I won't admit it.

I can't.

Not even to myself.

Liar liar.

CHAPTER SIXTEEN-LUC

A *virgin.*

"Luc, what are forecasts for this quarter?" Nico asks me.

I rumble through the numbers hardly paying any attention to them.

I don't have to. I know this shit by heart.

Days have passed since I've talked to her, touched her. I know it's fucking stupid.

I've been here every fucking day.

Holed up in my office like a snake in its den.

Waiting.

Watching.

Trying to catch up with what's going on inside me.

She had day shifts all this week, so it was a little

easier on me. But tonight is her first night shift and I'm all coiled up, ready to strike.

A fucking virgin.

This woman has me off fucking balance.

My pillow still smells like her. I wouldn't allow the cleaning service to wash it.

The sheets were stained with her virgin blood, and I was so fucking tempted to keep them.

But that would be sick.

Still should have kept them, my inner voice comments.

I wipe my hand over my face. Maria is haunting my every moment.

Asleep, I dream of her.

Awake, I think of her.

I need to know what she's hiding.

Well, you're not going to find that out in here, asshole.

My inner voice can be a real dick sometimes.

"Luc, what do you think?" Nico asks, and I make a noncommittal humming noise.

The discussion has moved on to other properties we have in development, and I half listen while our realtor gives us his report.

My job is to serve the king. That's why I got my law degree. That's why I do what I do.

All our dealings, legal or not, require thoughtful

inspection. Having a degree, or several, does not make me smarter than anyone else. But it makes me the right man to deal with some shit Nico simply doesn't have the patience for.

He is fine with letting me do that. So, I do. I handle the stuff he doesn't want to.

I use all my education, my expertise, what I know about the area where we choose to invest our hard earned money.

Sometimes it is a simple deal, sometimes we invade, depending on whether it's Viper Enterprises or simply the Vipers who are taking over.

You see, when you have an infestation of snakes, you either get rid of them or they rule.

The government didn't get rid of us.

The cops couldn't, or maybe they just wouldn't, because we cleaned up the streets they refused to.

We take care of people who come from the same place we did.

That's why we're in power and that's why we will remain in power because the real power is with the mob. The forgotten people on the fringes of society.

They need someone to look out for them, and that's what we do.

We provide for them.

The Vipers.

We keep the schools clean. We fund recreational centers, senior aid, and daycare.

We control the so-called government heroes.

Who do you think started the real epidemic hurting society? Who do you think allows the cartels, murderers, rapists, and worse to walk free just to get a deal done?

It is not us.

You cross a Viper, you get bit. Period.

We do bad things. I'm not saying we don't. But the way I see it, so does the government. Some of it is worse than anything we've ever done.

If anything, the Vipers have more ethics than most politicians I've met. And yes, I have met many.

It is simply part of the package, being a Princeton trained lawyer representing Viper Enterprises.

Every government everywhere in the world has their own issues. Their own slimy politicians, greasy dealings, and coverups. It's like they have their own morality.

And so do we. I'm not trying to say we're better. I'm just saying we're not all that different

A motherfucking virgin.

I'm trying to focus, but my brain can't stop thinking about it. Maria was untouched.

Completely fucking innocent.

I should feel bad, but I don't.

If anything, the fact she submitted willingly to me makes me want her even more.

She was a virgin, and me, I'm a tatted up, pierced fucking monster.

But the thing is, I don't think Maria is all white lace and halos. She has secrets. A past.

And I am dying to learn it. But my research on her is at an impasse. It seems Maria Mendoza only showed up on paper six years ago.

And I know what that means. But I need to know all of it.

A week has passed, and I haven't fucked her again. But I need to. Soon.

She's still keeping secrets. But I've been doing a little more digging and what I found isn't comforting.

Soon. I'll have the truth soon.

At least, that's what I tell myself.

"Yo, where's your head at?" Angel says.

I look up to find the realtor left, and Nico and Angel are just staring at me.

Nico seems amused. But Angel seems actually confounded.

I guess that makes sense. He is the muscle around here. Just like I told Baby Girl.

He's the muscle. I'm the brains. And Nico is the king.

He earned his crown fair and square, and the truth is, I don't want it.

I'm happy to serve the crown. Happy with my position.

Nico allows me to do my own thing. He doesn't care that I run my own investment firm, and that with my businesses I made tons of my own money.

He comes in with me on deals when he wants, and I am more than happy to share the wealth with him and Angel.

Nico also understands what drives me. He was there for me when my sister OD'd on the same junk that killed his mother.

He recognizes my pain, my need to exact my revenge on people I feel deserve it. And he is supportive.

Sometimes I use legal grounds. I've been responsible for the closing down of more than one laundering front.

All it takes is the right words in the right ears, a little envelope on the side, and bam.

Sure, there's always flat out war, but in war everyone loses. Nico and Angel joke that I am a pacifist.

It always makes me roll my eyes.

It's not that I'm not violent. Because I am.

I've killed people. I've hurt people. I've made threats after my sister died horribly in a dank alley, her body too weak to fight the poison her pusher stuck in her arm.

I was just a kid then, but it was Nico who helped me avenge her death.

We cleaned up that block. Got rid of the drug dealers who refused to monitor their product.

Now I do it without him. He has other deals to attend. The ports are important.

But I still see it as my personal mission to keep our old neighborhood streets clean.

So, yes, I employ my own guys, my own branch of Vipers to see to that.

Truth is, lately, it's not enough.

The same motherfucker who burned our warehouse is responsible for the recent influx of heroine laced with too much fucking fentanyl.

Sanchez Junior and his band of fucking morons.

I'm capable of things that maybe they don't even know, but now it seems I'm capable of something else.

Maria.

Virgin.

Mine.

I never knew I had it in me to feel this way about someone. But I feel it. For her.

Obsession.

Affection.

Infatuation.

Desire.

The likes of which I never thought possible.

"Earth to Luc," Angel persists.

These men are my family.

But I'm like two seconds away from cold cocking that fuck.

"Leave him alone, Angel. Luc has got things on his mind," Nico says, and he's grinning wider.

"Shut the fuck up," I grumble, but then I'm smirking, too.

"Yeah? It's been a while for you, bro. I think this calls for a drink," Angel says, getting up to round the small bar next to Nico's desk.

I roll my eyes but accept the tumbler of Whiskey Neat he holds out to me.

"What are we drinking to?" I ask.

"To the women who drive us wild," Nico says, and his gaze flicks to Angel who looks pensive at that toast.

Well, that's interesting.

I sip the dark, rich liquid and I nod.

Nico is definitely a good king.

He is just the right amount of unhinged and benevolent.

Maybe I should get his advice about Maria?

"Maria's worked for us for a while, bro, why now?" Angel asks.

"Because," Nico answers, "someone fucked with what Luc here claimed as his, even if only in his mind. He fucked with her, and it was time Luc let everyone know who she belonged to. Right?"

I look at the king, and my eyes widen. I dip my chin.

He's absolutely fucking right.

Maria is mine.

And someone did fuck with what's mine. And they did it here.

In my house.

Motherfucker.

Fury fills me, and it's a familiar old friend.

"What am I doing?" I rumble.

Instead of making sure everyone knows my woman is off fucking limits, here I am at the Den, in

Nico's office, on a Friday night, and she's out there, alone, working the bar.

Now, I'm mad at myself.

What the fuck am I doing, wasting time chatting with these two knuckleheads?

"Where you going?" Angel calls out as I walk to the door.

"To take my woman home."

CHAPTER SEVENTEEN-MARIA

I sense him before I see him.

When I look up from where I'm arranging a stack of cleaned glasses, I catch Luc rounding the bar.

"What are you doing?" I ask.

But he's not talking. His steel gaze combs over me from head to toe.

I'm wearing ripped up black jeans, my perfectly worn boots, and a gold tank top.

I am all out of the temporary coloring conditioner I use, so I have my hair in two braids, hoping to hide my natural highlights that have already started to show through.

I don't know what to do, so I just stand there.

"Luc?"

He exhales a breath and I see his chest move. It's the only thing that lets me know he's really there and not some figment of my imagination.

A week has passed since he brought me home with him. I haven't really talked to him since, though I've seen glimpses of him walking to his office.

Luc is a busy man. I know this, so I don't intrude.

Even though I want to.

I mean when a guy like that tells you that you're his you expect something.

But maybe those were just pretty words. Maybe my inexperienced fluffy ass just isn't good enough.

Those are just some of the ugly thoughts that've been twisting and winding around inside my brain.

But I push all of them away because he's here.

Right now, Luc is here. And he's staring at me like I'm a fucking piece of dark chocolate, the expensive kind with the soft cherry center.

I might be new to the whole sex thing, but my pussy doesn't know that.

It pulses and moisture wets my panties.

I take a moment to just stare at him. He's wearing a pale blue button down shirt, and I bite back my moan at the fact I can almost see his tattoos through the material.

His curls look glossy against his forehead, and the close crop beard he wears is trimmed.

His lips are in a hard line, but I know just how soft they feel, and a shiver runs through me at the memory.

Luc is not like other men. He is different.

Quiet.

Confident.

Commanding of all my attention.

He has that thing. Luc has *it*. Hell yes, he sure as fuck has it.

How could he not?

A man who looks like that could give Lucifer a run for his money. Then it hits me.

Luc. Lucifer.

Oh my fucking God.

Maybe he is the devil. Or maybe he's just named after him.

Either way, it is a fitting name.

The sparkle from his piercings dazzles me, and I want to lick them. To suck them into my mouth and taste the metal against his skin.

My throat goes dry.

Luc is just so, *so hot.*

His steel gaze trails down my belly, and it seems to narrow when he gets to the apex of my thighs.

Then he stalks forward and grabs my hand, pulling me back the way he came.

"Luc! What are you doing? I have to w-work," I stutter.

But if I think he will answer me, I have another thing coming.

It's too early for there to be much of a crowd. Antonio stares at me, eyes wide, but he says nothing.

And really, that's smart.

I don't think Luc is in any mood to discuss why he's dragging me out of the bar.

He leads me to his sleek car, rounds the hood to the passenger side, and opens the door.

I lick my lips, and he waits. Quietly.

So fucking quietly.

I huff a breath, then I sit. I look up and Luc dips his chin in approval.

His steel eyes sparkle like silver and those jet fighter planes are back.

For some reason, I am ridiculously pleased that I performed correctly. I hope he'll reward me.

Please, oh please.

I shouldn't feel that way. It's demeaning.

Only, I don't feel cheap. Under his silvery stare, I feel coveted.

And that warms me.

Luc is silent all the way to his renovated warehouse home, and I can't wait to get there.

His place is amazing.

We ride up the elevator in silence and I am not sure what to expect, but when we get through the door, he spins me around and pushes me back up against the door.

"Luc," I say, panting.

I'm so turned on and excited I don't know what to do.

He cups my pussy over my jeans, and I moan. Then he grabs my thighs and picks me up and I wrap my legs around him, mouth open, chest heaving.

"Give me that fucking mouth," he says, and crashes his lips to mine.

He grabs my braids, and he pulls back on them, but he doesn't allow me to lift my head. He is sucking on my tongue, and I might come from that alone.

His kiss is rough.

It is violent.

Desperate.

Needy.

So hot.

It is all the things I feel for him.

And I fucking love it.

I don't even notice that we're on the move. Luc carries me like I weigh nothing at all, and it makes me fucking swoon.

It's one of those *bigger girl secret wants* things.

Something we don't openly discuss because we don't want to be body shamed or laughed at.

But maybe we should talk about it.

Maybe we should stop apologizing for who we are and what we look like.

I mean, I don't think I need to beg for masculine attention. And I don't think anyone should have to.

I certainly won't say sorry cause I have a fat ass, a soft belly, and big tits. It's just how I'm made.

For fuck's sake, big girls need love, too.

For some of us, that means poetry and flowers.

And for others, it means we want to be swept off our feet.

Literally.

And preferably right before being fucked so hard we can't walk right for a few days.

Luc's big, pierced cock did a number on me. But maybe that was because it was my first time.

He was so tender and careful afterwards, I didn't mind at all.

In fact, all week long, I've missed it.

Him.

I have missed him.

Besides, I'm not a virgin now. And I can't wait for him to stretch me again.

"Tried to give you time to heal. I stayed away because I didn't want to tear up this hot little slit," he grunts as he tosses me on the bed.

Luc flips me onto my belly, and I moan. His hands are on me, He's tracing the rips in my jeans.

Suddenly, I feel something sharp, and I yelp.

"Did you just spank me?"

My pussy clenches. Moisture pools there, and I am stunned.

Do I like this? Should I?

It feels dirty.

But also good.

Very good.

Even better when he does it again and again, following each spank with a tender rubbing that leaves me begging for more.

"Luc," I beg, and I'm not sure I know what I am begging for.

"Wearing these fucking jeans. Showing everyone *my ass.* This is my ass, isn't it Baby Girl?"

Luc growls.

Motherfucking growls.

Like a beast.

And I am so turned on, I can barely think, much less speak.

So, I nod.

But that isn't good enough.

He spanks me again.

"I asked you a question. Is this *my ass?*"

"Y-yes. Yours," I whimper, and he rewards me by pressing the hard bar of his cock against the denim.

Fuck. I want him so badly.

"That's right. It's mine. All of you is mine."

He goes back to rubbing the bottom of my ass cheek, where that strategically placed tear reveals my flesh.

Then I feel his hands snake around to my fly. He pops the button and drags down the zipper.

Luc undresses me quickly. Then he flips me over again and my chest is heaving as he pulls the tank top over my head.

"So fucking perfect," he says.

My legs are clenched tightly together, but he is having none of that. With two hands on the soft, squishy flesh of my inner thighs, Luc pushes.

He wrenches them open, revealing my glistening sex.

I'm—I'm embarrassed. But I am turned on.

His steel gaze turns to molten silver as he just stares at me.

I am fully aware I am completely naked, and Luc is fully dressed.

Somehow, that makes it hotter.

"You keep those legs open, Baby Girl. That's it," he says, and his voice is so deep.

Rough with lust.

Savage with need.

And I know just how he feels.

I drop my legs wider.

I welcome him.

I need him.

Whatever he wants from me, I will give it to him.

Because even though I'm a liar about some aspects of my life, I am not a liar about this.

I belong to Luc Batiste.

His chest rumbles, and he says things to me. Filthy, dirty things about what he wants to do.

"Fuck, Baby Girl. Look at your dripping cunt. So fucking wet, aren't you? That dusky pink is so dark, so pretty. Pretty, pretty, pretty," he grunts, and I feel his need down to my toes.

Luc is so, *so big*.

Intense.

Commanding.

Simply more man than anyone I ever met in my whole life.

"Can't wait to stuff you with this cock. You like my dick, don't you? Love to feel me stretch you. Love it when my piercings rub inside you. Tell me."

I gasp and my pulse races. I nod.

"Good Girl. Gonna fuck you hard. Stamp myself inside you. Gonna tongue fuck this slit first."

Yes.

Fuck.

Please. Yes.

I want him to do everything he says.

His words stroke along my skin like hands.

"And it's mine. No one ever had this before. No one else will ever get to have it. Cause it's mine," he says, and I don't know if he is even talking to me anymore.

And I don't care. I am so amped.

By the time he moves, pressing his face right against the slick folds of my sex, I moan so loud, it reverberates off the walls.

Luc sucks in a great, big breath with his nose buried right in my pussy and I can't fucking move.

I never read or heard of anything like that, of men just breathing in the scent of pussy. But Luc is breathing in mine. And he seems to like it.

I pull on his hair, cause I can't take it anymore. Then he moves.

He lifts his head, a wicked grin on his handsome as fuck face.

"Want me to kiss this cunt, Baby? That what you want?"

"Please," I beg.

"Eyes on me, Baby Girl," he commands, and fuck, I can't help it, I listen to him.

Then he dives in. He eats me out with a ferocity I never experienced.

And I go wild.

CHAPTER EIGHTEEN-LUC

I never take off work, but I just spent the last forty-eight hours in my bed with Maria, only leaving to use the bathroom, shower, and eat.

I still haven't talked to her. I need to. I mean to.

But every time I look at her, my dick takes over.

The woman is a witch. A goddamn sorceress.

She has me completely captivated.

"It's ready," Maria calls from the kitchen where she insisted on making us something to eat, and I grin.

I get up from the sofa in the living room, where I just logged onto my laptop, and I walk to the kitchen.

The layout is open, so I have a view of everything she is doing.

Sunlight is streaming in from the huge windows, and I pause.

I haven't spent a lot of time with Maria outside in the daylight.

This is really the first time I've observed her in full sunshine.

And holy fuck.

She takes my breath away.

I never really notice because I'm over six feet, but Maria is tall for a woman. She has long, curvy legs that drive me insane.

I want to lick them.

Bite them.

I want to feel them squeezing me tight while I pull on her hair.

That fucking hair. It's so damn beautiful.

Her glossy hair is usually so dark, I thought it might be black.

But it's not.

It's a riot of colors this morning. A chestnut brown with dozens of lighter highlights running through it. They are every shade from gold to caramel to a burned sort of auburn.

I'm stunned. She's even more beautiful than I know.

Her almond-shaped eyes are a deep, velvet

brown. And she has short thick lashes, way darker than her hair, but still brown, circling them.

A couple of freckles dance across her nose and I'm dying to kiss them.

Her bottom lip is bigger than her top lip, but I know that already. I love how they feel when I kiss her.

Her skin is bronze and know it's just her because I've seen her naked and she has no tan lines.

The thought of her nude sunbathing runs through my brain, and I frown. But I shake it off.

She tucks a stray lock of hair behind her ears.

Fuck, my heart stutters inside my chest.

She looks so sweet. This is not the girl I think I know. The sinful and seductive one.

My throat closes. I can't speak even if I wanted to.

She is so stunning.

Gorgeous.

Mind-numbing.

I wonder why she uses whatever product that is that washes down my drain every time she shampoos her hair.

It's criminal. Her hair is too pretty to cover up like that.

But I'm not such a beast that I tell women what to wear or how to primp themselves.

Her back is to me, so she doesn't see me approach.

She's wearing my robe, and nothing else as she dishes up what smells like scrambled eggs and bacon.

My stomach rumbles, but my cock is already at half-mast.

Maria turns to me with a smile on her face, but it falters, and I cock my head.

"What's wrong?"

She licks her lips.

"Nothing, um, I didn't know you wear glasses," she murmurs.

Maria hurries to dish up the rest of the meal before handing me a plate. She's not looking at me, and her cheeks are dusky with embarrassment.

I grin wider. Then I touch her elbow and turn her to face me.

"You like my glasses? I look good to you, Baby Girl?" I ask, knowing she does by the way her dark, almond-shaped beauties seem to eat them up.

"Shut up, you know you look good," she says and rolls her eyes.

Who knew fucking glasses would be my woman's kryptonite?

I tuck away the information for later.

She pours me a cup of coffee, and I'm fucking delighted with how she readily hands me things. I want to reciprocate, so I do. I doctor her mug with cream and sugar, noticing her shocked smile as I hand it to her.

"You know how I take my coffee?"

I nod. But I don't tell her how I know. I don't say how I've spent hours memorizing her.

"Smells good," I say, trying to shake her out of her reverie.

"Oh? Thanks. Um, how did you know—"

"Eat your food, Maria," I tell her, and she listens, lifting her fork to her lips.

I watch her eat, and I am taken with the need to feed her. I don't know why.

It's something primal. A marrow deep need to provide for her.

I want to be the one to bring the food to her mouth. To slide it between her lips. To give her everything she needs.

I sit on those feelings.

It's too soon.

Too much.

I already took her virginity, something a monster

like me had no right to do. But now that I took it, I want all of her.

It's not enough. But I can't just keep her here.

I have work to do before Monday rolls around tomorrow, and she probably has things she needs to see to as well.

Right on cue, she brings it up.

"Um, I have to leave after this," she says,

"What? Why?"

Even though I was just thinking the same thing, I don't like that Maria brings it up first. Her leaving, that is.

I don't want her to go.

I want her in my house.

Right fucking here.

But I'm being crazy.

I mean, I want this woman like mad, but I can't just keep her here.

I want to.

But I can't.

What am I going to do? Lock her up like a prisoner. Or some kind of fucking caged bird.

Yessss, hisses my inner Viper.

I rub my hand over my face.

Shit.

Yeah, I really do want to.

But I can't. I just fucking can't.

And it is pissing me off.

"It's S-Sunday. I, *uh*, I go to church," she says, and I can't hide I'm stunned.

I'm over here getting all jealous, imagining a dozen fucking scenarios, all bad, and Sweet Baby Girl over here just wants to go to church.

I'm a complete asshole.

"Of course. I'll drive you home after we eat and get dressed, okay?"

She nods, her smile a little dimmer now, and that pisses me off.

But I'll make it up to her.

CHAPTER NINETEEN-MARIA

"Y ou're on at six, right? I'll send a car for you here at 5:30," Luc says, pulling up outside my apartment.

"What? No, you don't have to do that," I say, but he's just looking at me like *don't be stupid*.

So, I accept it.

After that minor uncomfortable moment at breakfast, Luc and I had a quick discussion about work and responsibilities.

He sometimes gets called out of town for the Vipers. And I totally understand and respect that.

Just like he understands I won't take money from him. I have to work. And if he won't let me work at the Den. Then I'll go elsewhere.

"Oh, really? Well, let me tell you right now the answer

is no. You fucking won't be tending bar anywhere else, Baby Girl. I want you right where I can see you. Where I can keep you safe. Got it?"

I hate to admit it, but I feel so relieved.

I mean, I want to be the kind of woman who can handle all her own problems. But mine are a little too big sometimes.

I need and want the protection Luc offers so freely.

Just like I want to keep doing whatever it is we are doing together. I wait as he rounds the car, opens my door, and helps me out.

I bite my lip, feeling a little silly with my borrowed sweatpants that are rolled up three times and my silky tank top.

But Luc looks at me like I'm a bombshell, so I push those feelings of inadequacy away.

"I'll see you tonight," he says, and he cups my neck and tugs me towards him.

I lean into his kiss, breathing in his masculine scent and savoring the feel of his strong arms all around me.

"Be good, Baby Girl."

"Always," I reply and grin.

Then I walk away, aware that he's watching every step I take.

My heart feels so full, and I almost don't see the envelope sitting on my floor.

I bend down to pick it up, but my mind is still stuck on Luc. He's not at all what I expected him to be.

I mean, he's every bit as smart as I assumed. But he's also intense, tender, and attentive.

Like really attentive.

Sure, I never did anything with a man before him. But I read books. And I had toys.

But no romance novel or vibrator ever got me off the way he did.

Luc is like a walking, talking miracle. His whole body is a work of art designed for one thing.

Good goddamn sex.

He is so patient with me. He guides me to heights I never imagined existed. And his words.

The guy I thought was quiet and judgy was a fucking general in the bedroom.

Or bathroom.

Or wherever.

Our escapades the last two days took us all over his luxurious warehouse turned loft home.

Escapades.

What an apt word. Being with him was a sensually erotic adventure I never even hoped for.

My entire body hums whenever I think of him, and those fighter jets inside my stomach go crazy whenever he is near.

I think I'm in love with him.

And it's with that thought in mind that I open the envelope.

Then all thoughts of Luc and love leave my brain.

My mother is in the hospital. And I can't stay hidden any longer.

Hang on, Mami.

CHAPTER TWENTY-LUC

I was still sitting in the car, just idling outside Maria's apartment building. Gathering my thoughts, as it were, when I happen to glance in my rearview mirror.

I see her. Maria. She looks harried. Frazzled. And she is running out the door.

She's still in my sweatpants, which placates me some. But I see she replaced the thin silk top with a t-shirt, and I know she must be sweating with the heat.

She's headed for the bus stop, but I'm not about to let that happen.

Heavy-handed?

Maybe.

But I can't seem to be anything but when it comes to this woman.

I put the car in reverse and step on the gas.

"Maria!"

I shout, and she turns her head, almond eyes swimming in tears.

She freezes, and it's like a switch goes off. I can see she's scared, and it makes me angry.

I want to know who is scaring my Baby Girl.

Who fucking dares?

I plan on getting answers, but first I need her in my car.

"Get in," I command, and like every time I issue an order, she obeys.

"What's going on?" I say without preamble.

Maria takes a breath, but she doesn't look at me. She faces forward, and I hate it.

It's like she's building a wall between us, and it makes me even madder.

"My mother is in the hospital. The Medical Center. Can you take me?" she asks, and her voice breaks at the last bit.

"Of course," I say, already putting the car in gear.

There's more. I know there is more.

But clearly, my woman is too fraught with worry

to handle a bunch of possessive male bullshit right now.

So, I shut my fucking mouth. And I drive.

She wipes at her face, and I grit my teeth. I reach over her, opening the glove compartment and grabbing the miniature box of tissues inside.

I hand them to her without saying a word.

Then she starts bawling. Great big sobs that shake her entire body, and I feel fucking helpless.

We're seven minutes out from the hospital.

And I can't stay quiet any longer.

CHAPTER TWENTY-ONE—MARIA

Tears blur my vision as Luc races as much as he can through Jersey City traffic to the Medical Center.

My mother's longtime friend and neighbor, Mr. Palermo, is the one who pushed that envelope through my door.

I'd given Mami my address and a burner phone to call, but I didn't have it with me the past few days.

I'm ashamed I missed her call, and that she had to resort to getting Mr. Palermo to find me.

It's just another reason I had to give up this charade.

"Easy, Baby Girl. Talk to me, tell me what's happening, please."

It's the please that does it. That, and Luc's big, warm hand pressing down on my thigh.

I hiccup and sniff, mopping my face with a tissue.

He's waiting for me to answer. His steel gaze is on my profile as we sit at a red light.

And I feel the weight of it. It's crushing me. Till it's not.

I look at him, and I decide. Now, his gaze is comforting me.

"You have to understand, this is hard for me. For so long, I-I haven't had anyone to trust," I confess.

"You can trust me, Maria. I will always take care of you," he says, and I feel those words wrap around my tiny, hopeful little heart.

I hope he's serious. That he won't hate me. But I know it's time I gave him something.

Besides my virginity, my inner voice snarks back at me.

"My mother has cancer."

"I am so sorry, Baby," he says and squeezes my leg.

The silence stretches, and the light turns green.

"I didn't know you had family here. Thought you were from out of town," he says, but I know he never believed that.

Not with my easily distinguishable Jersey accent.

"This last round of chemo is taking its toll. But I haven't been around much for her. I can't be," I whisper that last part.

"Why, Maria? Why can't you be there for your mother?" he asks.

"First, well, I'm from here, you know."

"From where?"

"New Jersey. I left six years ago after," I pause, sucking in a breath.

"Why?"

"I kinda had to. See, my father worked for a bad guy, and he was killed because of it," I confess.

"Who did he work for?" Luc asks.

But I can see in the way he's gripping the steering wheel he knows I'm not going to say something like Walmart.

"A drug dealer. Papi was his top enforcer."

Luc makes a dark, rumbling sound, and I know he is not happy.

"I was young, and it was all just normal. Just my everyday life. His odd hours. Having guns in the house. Strangers in and out. My parents were very much in love. Luc, my mother is the best person I know. If she didn't question it, I wasn't going to."

"Why did your father get killed?"

"I don't know. Everything was fine. Then, suddenly, it wasn't."

"And you came back here, to the Den, after six years on the run, for what? To trick us? To use me?" he asks, and it is like a knife through my heart.

"No! Luc, please! I need you to know I didn't ever plan this. I didn't plan us. Mami got sick, and I've been sending money. But this time, it's so much worse, and I had to come back. I'm scared I'll lose her."

I sneak a glance at Luc, and his eyes are on the road. If it wasn't for the slight twitch at the corner of his mouth telling me his jaw is clenched, I would think he had no feelings about this at all.

But he is mad. At me. And it hurts.

I know he has questions. But he bites his tongue.

He must be a phenomenal lawyer.

Unattached.

Steady.

Unemotional.

But it's killing me to see him so expressionless.

Still, and he knows how to listen. And suddenly it's like I can't stop talking.

"I, uh, I was *talking* to one of his boss' sons. Just flirting. It was all new. He got killed before my father. His two remaining sons were pissed off, and they blamed him. It was at my father's funeral that the younger brother decided I was his property."

Luc exhales, and it is ripe with disgust. I just don't know who it's aimed at.

But still, I continue.

All the guilt I feel for hiding and lying won't let me do anything else.

"He, um, he tried to, *you know*. So, that night, Mami and I made a plan for me to run. And I did. For six years. It seems stupid, but he scared me. He still drops in on my mother under the pretense of checking in on his father's old enforcer's widow. But I know that's not the reason," I whisper, even though saying it out loud makes me sound so weak and stupid.

He still doesn't talk, and we are just a few minutes away now.

"Luc, I know this looks bad," I say, desperate to explain my side.

"I know you think I was trying to get Nico's attention—"

"I don't want to know if you have feelings for Nico," he growls, and I see the vein in his forehead throbbing.

"No! I don't have any feelings for him at all! I mean, I respect him. And Anna is becoming my friend now, so, I like the fact that he's good to her. But Luc, I never felt like this about him," I blurt.

"Felt like what?" he asks, and I am trapped once more in his steel gaze.

"You know," I whisper, but he doesn't let me off the hook.

Maybe it's the lawyer in him.

Or the viper.

Maybe they are both the same thing.

Predator.

Merciless.

Devious.

Cunning.

Luc is watching me, and I think he's looking to see if I tell another lie.

But I am through with them. I haven't got any left in me.

I know I should have kept my mouth shut. But it's too late now.

"Maria, what did you mean when you said you never felt like this about Nico?"

The temperature in the car seems to jump ten degrees and I am sweating and uncomfortable, still cloaked in his way too long sweatpants that manage to cling to my ass but fall off my waist.

Shit.

This is really not how I imagined this conversation to go.

"You really want to ask me that now?" I ask, feeling raw and wrung out as he pulls into a parking spot in the Medical Center garage.

"Yes."

That's all the reply he offers. And it seriously pisses me off.

"Fine. You wanna know? I'll tell you then."

I turn my face, so I am looking at him. His expression is completely blank, and my nostrils start flaring.

I'm so fucking mad.

"I feel like maybe I am in love with you, you jerk!" I shout that last bit.

Then I open the door without waiting for him, and I slam it in his stupid handsome as fuck face.

Fuck this man.

How dare Luc put me through that when I'm worried about my mother! When I'm feeling so vulnerable and scared.

How fucking dare he!

I don't look back. I just storm away.

But I should have known he wouldn't let me get away with that, either. He grabs my arm and spins me around, then he cups my face and slams his lips to mine.

This man.

I swear to Christ every time he kisses me it's like he is branding me. I want to push him away.

But I don't. I can't. Because I do love him.

It's reckless. Idiotic, really. But I do.

"You say you love me then you walk away from me, Baby Girl? No. Never," he says and wraps one arm around my waist, pulling me into his hard body.

Walls of muscle wrap around me, and I cry.

"I won't let you do that, Maria. Not ever. I can't fucking stand it when you walk away from me," he grunts, and he's kissing my cheeks now.

God.

He's licking my tears away now.

Drinking them in.

Savoring them.

He groans, and I sway on my feet. But he is there, holding me up, and I am so fucking grateful.

I cling to Luc in the hot, damp garage, absorbing his strength, leaning on him.

"I got you."

He does have me.

I really think he does.

"Come on. Let's go see your mother," he says.

And I follow like a docile lamb.

Like his good Baby Girl.

I want to be his so damn bad.

CHAPTER TWENTY-TWO-LUC

"Mia, you didn't have to come here," her mother says, and I note the name she's using.

It's not Maria.

I frown.

Clearly, we have more secrets to clear up, but we'll get to it. Maria said she's in love with me. And because of that, I need to know everything.

Every. Single. Fucking. Thing.

There is no way I am letting her go now. So, yeah, we will get to it.

I am going to discover everything about her.

I have to.

There is no other choice.

Not for me. Not for her.

I watch the two women embrace, and my gaze flits to the older man sitting beside the bed.

He has to be the mother's age, though it is hard to tell with her illness.

I can see the resemblance. Maria's mother must be a gorgeous woman when she's well.

But now, she is thin and pale. Her head is covered in a colorful silk scarf, and she has on her own robe.

The man nods at me. A sign of respect. And I give him the same acknowledgement.

"We've been here two days, and the doctor still hasn't seen her himself," he rumbles.

I immediately start texting out orders to my guys. That kind of thing will not be tolerated.

Anyone important to Maria is now important to me.

Whoever sent her running, well, I'll deal with him, too. As soon as she gives me a name.

"It's gonna be okay, Mami," Maria tells her mother.

"Will you have to leave now? I want you safe, Mia, but I miss you so," she cries.

"I'm not leaving you, Mami. I promise."

The older woman simply cries, holding her daughter's hand, and it tugs on my heartstrings.

Damn fucking straight, she's not leaving.

Maria is telling her mother not to worry, and she isn't lying. I've already set things into motion. I want her, *Celia Lopez*, I note the name, to be seen by the top oncologist at the hospital.

Viper Enterprises has donated plenty of money to this place, as have I, personally.

My name has clout, and I am not afraid to use it. I hear some of my guys arrive. The team leader's name is Otto. He sticks his head in the door and nods at me, telling me they're in place.

Maria's mother is getting round-the-clock security while she is here, and a personal fucking escort back to her house when she is released.

The doctor arrives a few minutes later.

He looks harried and a little afraid when he sees me, and I know why. I just had one of my guys *motivate him* to bump Celia Lopez up on his list of patients to see.

"Ah, um, hello, Mrs. Lopez, I'm Dr. Xavier. Let's see what your chart says, shall we?"

Celia nods at the doctor, and Maria blinks up at me. She mouths the words *thank you*. And I dip my chin.

She doesn't have to thank me. Not for this. This is just common fucking courtesy.

I get it. Hospitals are full of overworked staff.

Hours are nuts. And there are not enough nurses and doctors to go around.

But their patients are real people. They deserve care and consideration.

I decide I want better for Maria's mother. I want the top oncologist in the whole fucking state to look at this woman's records.

As for the Medical Center, I make a note to donate a full ten years' worth of salaries for ten more oncology nurses to be added to the staff. Maybe that will help.

"Would you mind excusing us so I can do an exam?" the doctor says, and he looks two seconds from shitting himself.

I nod and send a small wink to Maria before exiting. The neighbor follows me.

"Joe Palermo," he says, holding out his hand as we move to the foot of the bed, backing away a few more feet while the woman gush and sob and embrace.

"Luc Batiste. You her neighbor?" I ask.

"Yeah. I lived next to the Lopez family, thirty-five years. I saw Mia, *er*, Maria, be born. She came too quickly for Celia to make it to the hospital. Delivered her right on the lawn. The husband was out," he says, and I pick up on his sneer.

Something clicks, and suddenly, I know this guy. Not him, per se. But I know what he is.

I can smell it on him.

Joe Palmero is a cop. Or he was.

"You know who I am?" I ask quietly.

The older man looks me in the eye, and he nods.

"How did you find Maria?" I say.

"Looked through Celia's wallet. She collapsed in the garden, and I brought her here. Been trying to call *Maria* for two days. Was she with you?"

I raise an eyebrow. It's nice he's protective of her.

But I'm not confirming or denying shit to him. It is none of his damn business.

"Look, I get it. I was on the job a long time. Emiliano Lopez wasn't a good man. He loved his wife and daughter, though. I will give him that. But he worked for a fucking monster. I just wanna know, you gonna protect her?"

I consider his words carefully.

Of course, I am going to protect her.

Maria is mine. That isn't a question.

But I need to know more, and I'm not sure how far to push her just yet.

A woman like her doesn't fall in my lap every day. She certainly doesn't tell me she's in love with me.

I'm already fucking obsessed with her.

But now, well, now it's no contest. I will burn this whole fucking city to the ground if some soon to be dead prick doesn't get the message that Baby Girl, *and yeah that is what I am going to call her until she tells me which is her real fucking name or until I decide what to call her*, is mine.

When I say burn it tot he ground, I fucking mean it.

Metaphorically or literally.

I'll destroy it all. It makes no difference to me.

Nico is the king of the Vipers, and my blood brother. He is the most unhinged fucker I know. I'm not the king.

But I am the Council. And he's not the only one of us who can get shit done.

I might look like I don't do violence, but I'm no stranger to it.

No, I don't talk a lot. I don't like to waste words. But that doesn't mean a fucking thing.

I've got my own methods and means.

So, when I say I will fucking burn this city to the ground, I mean I will rain destruction down on any motherfucker who terrorizes my woman.

I protect what's mine.

And that woman is irrefutably mine.

"She'll be safe. Her mother, too," I tell good ol' neighbor Joe.

He exhales audibly. But I'm not done with him yet.

"Now, tell me the name of that *monster*."

CHAPTER TWENTY-THREE-LUC

*E**nrico Sanchez.*
I breathe in sharply and turn the AC on in my car. It's hot as hell outside.

Even the harsh antiseptic air inside the hospital was better than this damp, smothering heat.

Enrico motherfucking Sanchez.

A fiery rage builds up inside of me, and it's directed at the woman I am pretty goddamn sure I am in love with.

Fuck.

I know it's unfair. But I can't help it. Just like I can't help how I feel about her.

Maria has been lying to all of us for months. I knew that.

Sure, she's good at her job. She fits in with the staff, but there was always just something else about her.

I've watched her so goddamn closely, but how the fuck did I miss this?

How did I miss her fear? Or the fact she was running from something?

My temper spikes and I punch the steering wheel, sending off a blast of the horn.

I have to consider all the possibilities. If it is Sanchez she is running from, I will kill that piece of shit myself.

But there is another possibility, and just thinking about it makes me sick to my stomach.

What if Maria, or fucking Mia, whatever her name is, is just playing a game?

I shake off that thought immediately. Whatever trouble she is in, Baby Girl can count on me to help.

The city blurs by and I run two lights before I calm the fuck down.

And I realize I don't fucking care what her sins are. I will take care of it. Of her.

"Yeah," I say, connecting the incoming call from via Bluetooth.

It's Otto. He's still in the hospital guarding Maria

and her mother, but I gave him another job as well. One he could perform with a few phone calls.

"Mr. Batiste? We ran the check on that guy from the bar fight."

"And?" I say, annoyed at the delay.

"He's a foot soldier for Sanchez,"

"Fuck!" I roar. "She still there?"

"No, she left with Smith as per your instructions. He texted a few minutes ago. She is inside her apartment, getting ready for work. He will drive her to the Den as soon as she surfaces," Otto says.

"I want all updates in real time on the fucking phone, got it?"

"Yes, sir."

I click end and pull into the alley behind the Den.

I was going to wait until I spoke to her before I went to Nico and Angel and explained what was going on.

I hate not having all the details. But this conversation is overdue and now it is unavoidable.

If either surviving Sanchez brother has been stalking my woman, he's a dead man.

But I owe Nico my loyalty, and, on this thing, I might also need his approval.

It irritates me.

But I get it.

I understand. And it is only because of my love and respect for the two men that I am not waiting in a dark room somewhere to slit that Sanchez motherfucker's throat.

CHAPTER TWENTY-FOUR-MARIA

I know something is wrong.

I told Luc a lot today, so I expect him to be distant.

But I don't expect him to ice me out.

I've sent three texts so far, but he's not returned a single one.

Too many tears have been shed today already, and I just don't have any more to give.

The good news is my mother's case is being taken over by the head oncologist, and he is consulting with one of the top doctors in the state.

Amazing, right?

Someone pulled strings. Made promises. Or threats. And honestly, either is fine.

I just want Mami to get better. And for the doctors to pay attention to her.

It's finally happening now. All because of Luc.

If I didn't already love him, that would have probably done it.

I dress with care, pulling on a long skirt with a slide slit and a shimmery silver blouse with tiny silver hooks in the front.

It is loose and sleeveless. I have it tied at my waist and opened the first two hooks to reveal hints of my black bra.

I've worn this outfit before, and it gives me a confidence boost. The top emphasizes my breasts and not my stomach. And the skirt is stretchy, the slit makes it easy for me to move around.

Outside, the same driver is waiting for me, and he opens the rear door when I approach.

He doesn't speak and I don't expect him to. I just nod my head and thank him when I get inside.

Nerves have me gripping the fabric of my skirt, and I force myself to let go. I close my eyes and take a calming breath in through my nose. Exhaling through my mouth, I open my eyes and I feel a modicum better.

He pulls up to the back, and I frown.

I mean, I've been this way a few times, but I usually enter through the front of the bar.

"Ma'am?" the driver says, and I turn to see him standing there, door open, looking at me like I have eight heads.

"Ma'am? I'm twenty-seven," I scoff, but he just shrugs his massive shoulders.

"Just call me Maria," I say, and he's looking at me like I'm nuts.

Then, he's averting his gaze, and it's probably because the crazy fuck behind me is glaring at him.

"Like hell he will," Luc says, and I gasp as he steps right up to me, pressing his hard body into mine.

My knees are positively weak, and my blood sizzles when I feel him, so hard and heavy, against me.

"Luc," I say, and I lean my head back, hoping he will take the hint and kiss me.

His nostrils flare slightly, and I can feel the hum inside his throat as it reverberates through his chest.

He steps back, and I moan at the loss.

"We have things to talk about."

I nod.

"After work?" I ask.

But Luc doesn't answer, he walks away, leaving me to follow.

There is only one door, so it's not like I have a choice.

CHAPTER TWENTY-FIVE-LUC

My blood is roaring inside my ears, and I can't even fucking think, much less form words.

I feel like a wounded beast.

I just finished my meeting with Nico and Angel, and I am fucking two seconds from losing it.

I take in Maria's sexy outfit.

Her dark almond eyes and thick black lashes.

That fucking honey lilac scent.

And I want to howl like an animal. But vipers don't fucking howl. And I'm not just Luc here.

I'm the motherfucking Council.

I replay the last few minutes of the meeting as I lead the way to my office.

"Uh, Boss, there is something else."

"What?" Nico asks.

"Maria. She's been hiding something"

"And?"

"I don't know, Nico. But that scuffle the other day? The guy I fucked up is a scout for Sanchez," I tell him.

"So, you think Maria is working for Sanchez?"

"I don't know," I tell him, and it guts me.

"We had Maria vetted like everyone else," Angel says.

I hear her boots padding behind me and I grit my teeth.

She looks good. Really good.

All I want to do is sink into her. But fucking Baby Girl is the last thing I need to do right now.

And it makes me so angry.

"Sit down, *Mia*."

I am seated at my desk and facing her when I say her birth name, and she fumbles a step.

But she's not a coward and despite what she thinks, she is not weak.

She straightens her shoulders and takes another step. Then another. Then she sits at one of the chairs in front of my desk.

I don't want her there. I want her on my lap.

But I need answers.

And I am done being patient.

"Do you work for Sanchez?" I ask, acknowledging the big, ugly fucking elephant in the room.

"What?" she gasps, and I see confusion and then anger fill her gaze.

"You think I work for that piece of shit? I told you, I flirted with his son when I was barely twenty-one. He died before anything got serious, as you should fucking know!" she shouts.

I'm equal parts enraged that she mentions this youthful flirtation, and so fucking proud of her for yelling at me.

"Why didn't you tell me who your father worked for when you told me your story earlier today?"

She looks at me like she doesn't know what I'm talking about, then she shakes her head.

"I don't know, Luc. I mean, I was falling apart before. Mami was in the hospital, and I felt guilty about not knowing because I was at your place with you. Then you, you tricked me into saying I love you, and that stressed me out!"

Maria is shouting at me, and fuck, she looks so good.

Her tits are heaving, and I want to fall face first into them. Her eyes are shining, her hair is wild and floating around her shoulders, and the vibe she is giving off is pure fucking power and heat.

"I tried telling you everything, but it's a fucking lot! I wasn't lying about it, Luc," she is still shouting.

This woman has the power to fucking wreck me.

Does she know it?

Does she care?

The idea she is playing me for a fool. That she is using me to get Sanchez closer to taking over the Vipers' turf is driving me mad.

But I still want her so fucking badly, I can taste it.

She'll make a fool of you, something dark whispers inside me. But I shut that thought right fucking down.

I stand and I wipe my hand across my desk, sending pens and papers flying.

"How the fuck am I supposed to know what you're lying about if you keep things from me?!"

It's my turn to be mad.

Fuck.

And I am mad. I'm so fucking mad.

But Maria grabs the handles of the chair, jumping because I startle her with my anger.

Mia not Maria.

"Maria's my middle name. It's still mine," she whimpers, and I close my eyes.

"I didn't know I said that out loud," I murmur.

"Luc," she says, standing, and she walks over to me, her hands outstretched.

I shake my head.

I can't let her touch me. If she touches me I will fuck her right here,

But she can't hear my inner arguments.

"Fuck," I hiss as she smooths her hands up my chest.

"What are you doing?" I growl.

"Whatever I want," she replies.

And it's so hot.

Her eyes are heavy-lidded as she drops to her knees in front of me.

My dick is pounding against my pants, and I groan as she slides the zipper down and reaches into my boxers, freeing me.

"I'm not a spy, Luc. I wouldn't even know how to start," she says, then kisses my tip.

"It's true, I came here with a plan to get protection. But I guess I'm just as naïve as I used to be. I didn't plan for you. I didn't know I would fall for you," she says, and wraps her tongue around the ring dangling from the tip of my cock.

"Maria, you are playing with fire," I growl, unable to resist flexing my hips as she wraps her mouth around me.

"I've never done this. But I want to try. Will you t-teach me?" she whispers and she's using both hands to circle the base of my dick.

I nod.

"Open wide, Baby Girl. That's it. Stretch that fucking mouth. Loosen your jaw, that's it. Now keep your eyes on me. Watch me as I feed you my dick."

I'm not exactly sure how we went from having an argument where Luc basically accused me of being some sort of criminal underworld spy to him shoving his cock in my mouth.

But I have to admit.

I like it.

Ever since we started whatever this thing is between us, I'd been reading up on my smut. I've also been checking out some porn. Trying to gain perspective on how to fuck a man with so many delicious piercings.

His cock glitters and glows with metal in the dim lighting, and it's like I'm hypnotized. The sites I visited say piercings are pleasurable for him and her.

So I pay attention to each one. Licking and

sucking them before I try to take his dick into my throat.

I gag a few times. Teardrops are rolling down my cheeks.

But I'm trying. And Lucy is praising me. His dick is getting harder, and I moan around as much of him as I can fit.

Christ, I am so damn wet.

"Godfuckingdamn, Baby Girl. Get up, bend over."

He drags me up with his hand on my hair and slams his lips to mine before practically shoving me as he turns and positions me across his desk.

Luc lifts my skirt, and I moan.

"You left the house in that?" he groans, and I smile with my face pressed against his beautiful waterfall desk.

I know what he sees. I am wearing a pair of mesh and lace backless panties. Basically, my entire ass is on display, but you can see a band of lace around my waist and some elastic by my thighs.

And there's a little bow right on top, and if he chooses, well, Luc can slide his dick right inside me without having to tear them off or anything.

Okay, so the story behind them is I bought them at a coworker's lingerie party a couple of years ago when I was living in Maryland.

No, I have never worn them before. I never had a reason to.

And I swear, I was not going to buy them, but the woman selling them had this impressive speech about lingerie being empowering for women.

She said something about how women can project a more confident demeanor if we felt more confident from the inside out.

Lingerie can change your life.

Her words, not mine.

I never thought it was possible before. But I must admit. Ever since I put them on, I've felt different.

Sexy.

Desired.

Powerful.

But Luc's groan is enough to make me feel ten times better than I did before.

"Fuck, Baby Girl. Look at that ass. Goddamn," he grunts.

His big rough hands are squeezing and kneading my flesh. I moan, pushing back when I feel his fingers delve between my dripping folds.

"So wet. So fucking hot," he murmurs.

Luc is running his digits through my slick, pressing them against my asshole.

I gasp.

"You're so fucking perfect. I can't wait to fuck you everywhere," he groans, notching his dick just inside my entrance.

It's only been hours, not days, since we fucked. Just that morning, in fact.

But this time, Luc knows the truth about me.

This time, there are no lies. Only us.

He flexes his hips, driving that decked out dick of his all the way inside me. And I feel it all.

Every barbell and ball.

Every inch of his monster cock's girth.

And I want it. I want all of it.

"Luc!" I yell his name.

"That's right, Baby Girl. Say my fucking name. Scream it," he grunts, pulling my hair back so my face lifts off the desk.

But he doesn't let any other part of me move.

He pounds into me, his pace punishing.

"Tell me who owns this body. Say it."

"Luc owns it! Oh, God. Yes," I whimper.

My legs are shaking.

Thank God for Luc and the desk holding me up.

Heat starts inside my core. A fiery thrill of feeling writing around, teasing my clit. And I need more.

As if he senses it, Luc's hand snakes around my

hip. The feel of his pants against my bare thighs only heightens the sensations rolling through me.

"Goddamn, these panties are fucking perfect," he grunts, finding the slit in front, and delving inside the fabric so he can access my aching clit.

Three rubs and I explode. The sound coming out of me is something else. It's inhuman.

But it must be okay because it seems to send Luc right over the edge.

Hot cum fills me, and it feels so good.

Is that normal?

I mean, should I like the way his cum feels leaking out of me?

I feel him lean back, but his hand is on my back, keeping me where I am.

"W-what are you doing?"

Then his fingers are there as his dick slides out of me. Luc is gathering his cum and pushing it back inside my cunt.

"You look so fucking hot, Baby Girl, dripping with my cum."

I squirm and try to move. But he's still looking. And I'm not sure what to do.

"Stay there," he says, and I listen.

I always listen when we're like this and Luc gives me an order.

I can't help it.

It's the most liberating feeling I have ever had. And I really want that feeling to remain.

I want both.

Freedom.

Him.

I want it all.

"That was," I say, after he cleans me up and puts my skirt back in place.

"Yes, it was," he grins and kisses me on the lips.

No matter what, I am never prepared for Luc's kisses.

They are always equal parts seduction and desperation, and I am officially addicted to them.

"Let's go."

"Where?"

"You said you want to work, so come on," he opens the door.

"You're coming to the bar. You never do that."

I should know. For months, I've been curious about him. Nico and Angel always make appearances on the floor.

But Luc never does.

Well, not until recently.

"Get a move on, Baby Girl. After your shift, we have to go get somethings from your apartment."

One thing I have learned about him is Luc is incredibly bossy. I mean, I get it, he's rich and powerful and educated. And he is damn well used to getting his way.

It shouldn't be sexy. But like everything else with him, it is.

His walk is determined, and his path straightforward.

I've gotten used to him leading me around like a puppy. But he is not doing that now.

He has me tight to his side. And I like it.

"What things do we need from my apartment?" I ask.

"Some clothes for you. Your toiletries. Stuff like that."

"What? Why?"

He opens the bar hatch and I walk through, still not understanding as he follows me.

Antonio gets out of our way, and I move to my usual side of the bar.

"Didn't I tell you?" Luc says, grabbing the stool I sometimes use when taking a break and leaning his hip against it as he faces the growing crowd.

"You're moving in with me."

CHAPTER TWENTY-SEVEN-LUC

"Luc, this is crazy," Maria says, and I know she's just nervous.

But my mind is made up.

"And I'm crazy about you, so it makes sense," I tell her, and I feel her eyes on me.

I know she needs more.

She's told me she loves me, and all I say is I'm crazy about you?

Fucking lame, Luc.

I grit my teeth. My inner voice can be a total douchebag sometimes.

"What if you regret this? What if you get tired of me in like a day?"

"Just keep wearing those backless panties and we

won't have a problem," I mumble and adjust my hardening dick.

She smirks. But then she shakes her head.

"I'm serious, Luc," she replies as I pull into the garage.

I turn in my seat and grab her chin.

"I'm fucking serious too. You belong to me, Baby Girl. Now keep your sweet ass right there until I open the door," I say, then I lean over and kiss her lips.

Goddamn.

I love kissing Maria. It's an addiction, I know.

Each time our lips meet, I want to swallow her down.

I want to devour her so I can keep her inside me, always.

She doesn't know it. She can't comprehend it.

Seven months is a long time to obsess over someone. I know her better than she thinks. I know she fits perfectly with my life.

So yeah, I am very certain I want her living in my house.

Our house now.

I grin at that and open her door, cocking my head as I watch her long skirt get caught on something. It slides up as she moves forward, then it slips back down her thick thighs as she stands.

Fuck.

Who knew getting out of a car could rival pornography?

On a hotness scale of one to ten, I give Baby Girl an eleven. And knowing that I'm the only man to have her, well, that just makes it even better.

What can I say? I'm a fucking barbarian like that.

I go to the trunk and take out her scuffed up rolling suitcase and the backpack she filled with her toiletries.

"Um, what about my other stuff?" she asks.

"It'll be packed up and brought over," I tell her.

"That's silly. I can do it."

"Not necessary," I say.

I won't tell her I can't stand the idea of her in that place.

Basement apartment? The landlord should be shot.

It's a fucking hovel.

Oh, she did what she could to brighten it. She has woven baskets and bins, colorful curtains hanging up.

It's not her. It's the place. The landlord is more like a slumlord, and I plan to have words with him.

Maria isn't the slob she claims she is.

Okay, there is some disarray with clothes and makeup. But everything beneath it, the stuff that matters, it is all clean.

Which is saying a lot, considering the floors and cabinets and appliances all suck.

Fucking shit hole.

Maria will not be returning to that dump. Period.

The elevator opens silently, and I place my hand on the lock, then instruct her to do the same.

"There, now you are in the system. And all my men already know who you are and that you live here now."

She nods, but she's worrying her lip between her teeth.

I know she's been here, but I admit, I didn't exactly give her a tour.

"Let me show you upstairs," I say to break the ice.

"Don't we need to use the elevator?" she asks, likely because I am tugging her in the other direction.

"Yeah, but it's a different one."

Her eyebrows raise and I rub the back of my neck.

She's quiet while we ride up, and I don't pressure her, cause I am generally a quiet person, too.

I've seen her apartment now, and I think she'll like what I am going to show her.

"What's this?" she asks, pointing to the door that leads to a set of stairs.

"That goes to the roof, but come in here first," I tell her.

She listens, as she usually does, and my heart beats faster.

I fucking love how she trusts me. She might not know it. Hell, maybe she is too young to know it.

But I push that thought out of my head. I'm more than ten years her senior, and that is something I really don't want to dwell on.

Besides, Maria is not like other women. She's graceful and smart.

Hardworking.

Sweet.

And dirty.

For a recent inductee into the world of carnal delight, Maria is a goddamn prodigy.

Her willingness to follow my lead makes that hard heart inside my chest pump a little harder. She makes my blood sizzle and my body ache.

She's so damn beautiful. Sometimes it hurts to look at her.

All that innocence. All that willingness to follow

me into sin. It is irresistible. So, I don't bother trying.

And the thought of not being with her? It breaks my fucking heart.

So, I won't entertain it.

Cause it is not going to happen.

CHAPTER TWENTY-EIGHT- MARIA

Wow.

Luc flips a large metal handle and then he slides what I soon realize is a refurbished barn door.

It's stained black. True black. But done expertly so you can see the wood grain beneath it.

It's fucking superb, and it matches the hall and other doors on this level. Again, I am awestruck by how huge this place is.

"Baby Girl?" he says, and I turn my head away from the door.

And I am floored.

"Are these all yours?" I ask stupidly, because it is his house, so obviously the answer is yes.

"Uh huh," he replies, a sexy as hell grin spreading wide as he watches me take it all in.

The room is big. Huge. Bigger than my whole apartment.

There is an enormous replica of Luc's waterfall desk, but this is more like a table. The design is the same though. And it is beautiful.

A couple of deep-seated leather chairs surround the table. All of it sits on an elegant rug that covers the center of the hardwood floor.

Near a large window, there is a comfortable-looking chaise loveseat, and I can just imagine lying there with a soft throw blanket.

Maybe I can get Anna to quilt one for me.

Recessed lights are scattered across the ceiling in various sizes, and I wonder if the color is voice controlled.

There are also half a dozen floor lamps and a fireplace near the chaise lounge.

I notice a small rolling door that is sitting open, revealing a sort of hidden pantry with a sink, a coffee machine, a few bottles of wine and top shelf whiskey, and a mini fridge on the bottom.

I grin at that.

But all these are not the showstoppers.

Oh no.

That prize belongs to the hundreds, if not thousands, of books filling the floor to ceiling, wall to wall wooden bookshelves that are all finished with that same black stain.

"Do you like it?"

"Like it? I feel like Belle," I whisper, twirling around to try to take them all in.

"You calling me the Beast?" Luc asks from right behind me.

I feel his hands on my hips, and I moan and lean back.

"This is all yours now, Baby Girl."

"Luc," I snort. "You can't mean that."

"Of course, I do. Everything I have is yours now," he tells me.

"Why? Why would you do that?" I ask, and I turn slowly.

True, I've told Luc that I love him. But he's never said it back.

I know it shouldn't matter. That the truest love is unconditional. And I love him. Honestly and truly with every bit of my heart.

But he's moved me into his home without saying those three little words. With no real explanation at all. And now he's telling me this is all mine, too.

So, I need to know.

Does he love me?

"Why Luc?" I repeat, and his steel-eyed stare pins me in place.

"Because you belong to me, *Mia Alejandra Maria Lopez*. Daughter of Emiliano and Celia Lopez."

I gasp.

He knows my real name.

The one I tried so desperately to hide for six long years. And it is mine, but then again, it's not. I'm not Mia anymore. I'm not sure who I am, really. But I know one thing.

I am his.

I swallow back a sob before I can speak.

"You ran a background check on me?" I ask, and my eyes fill with tears.

He nods.

His silver piercings sparkle in the light streaming in from the huge window. His steel eyes are glittering too, matching the color, and I swear he looks just like Lucifer then.

The Vipers aren't ugly. I mean, Nico and Angel are good looking men. But they don't hold a candle to my man. No one does.

Is he my man? Can this be real?

I sniff. My tears start to flow.

And I'm not sure if they are happy or sad tears as they spill over.

I'm aware I've told lies. I had to, but that doesn't make it right.

Luc is a powerful man, and he can't afford to make mistakes. He has to be sure of me, and I understand how it looks to anyone on the outside.

Me with my connection to the Sanchez brothers and him with his ties to the Vipers.

So yeah, I understand his need to run a background check. He has a lot of people to protect.

I want to be one of them. And more, I want to protect him, too.

Some women give their men safe harbor, but I don't know if I am the type to sit home and wait.

Sure, I want to mean something to him. I love him.

But I can give him more than a soft place to land. I can give him support. I can help him with the burdens he bears.

I can and I will.

If he lets me.

"I had to run it, you understand?" he asks, and I nod, incapable of speech.

"But I ran one on me too. For you. And you can have it, Maria. I will willingly give it to you. But if you want to know anything, Maria. Just ask me. Ask me and I'll tell you."

I bite my lip and warmth fills me. Those jet fighter pilots in my stomach are revving their engines.

I know he just told me the reason he's brought me here.

Because I am his.

And I know it should be enough. I want it to be enough.

My heart squeezes.

The truth is, I want more from Luc than to share his bed and his home.

I want more than to just belong to him. I want him to belong to me too, but I don't know how to ask for that.

Some people don't know how to love.

Maybe he will someday.

I can dream, can't I?

CHAPTER TWENTY-NINE-LUC

I smirk as the first few notes from Poison's *Every Rose Has Its Thorn* begin to play across my sound system and I shake my head.

Maria certainly has eclectic taste.

"I love this song!" She shouts from the living room and starts to sing.

Badly.

But I fucking love it.

The final delivery of Maria's stuff arrived two days ago, and I have to admit, the woman has more shit than I ever imagined.

We've been unpacking all day. She's wearing a pair of shorts that I'd spank her ass for if she tried to leave the house with them, but I have to admit I don't hate how she looks every time she bends over in them to grab another knick-knack from one of the eight boxes of stuff my guys removed from her apartment.

I grin as I pick up one of the seventeen shot glasses, she has in the box marked kitchen.

This one says Dallas, Texas. There's one with big glass boobs on it that says Fort Lauderdale. And another with the Statue of Liberty etched into it.

"What?" she asks, grinning as she snatches it out of my hand.

"You, uh, seem to like shot glasses," I say.

"They're the cheapest souvenir you can buy when you're in a new city and they fit perfectly in a carry-on bag."

She gets quiet then and takes the rest of them out, loading them into the dishwasher.

Something about the memory subdues her, and I curse under my breath and tug on her arm.

This is the side of her I've been wanting to know for months.

The Maria I used to watch on my security feed is cocky and arrogant.

Someone might call her wanton or promiscuous when she's working, teasing customers, and smiling at them. But I know that's always been an act.

A show. Like she is putting on a costume every time she gets behind the bar.

Yeah, I've watched her flirt. It's killed me watching her flirt, but she wasn't mine then.

Not like she is now.

Fine.

I'm a possessive prick.

But I won't compromise on this.

I don't want her working in the bar anymore. It's going to be one of my stipulations of our arrangement.

I know we've been over it before. But she doesn't have to worry about money.

Maria can pursue anything she wants to do now. She can go back to school. Start a business.

Anything at all.

Yeah, I'm aware it makes me a dick. I know I shouldn't demand it.

But I can't fucking help myself.

My girl isn't gonna work at the bar. No fucking way.

My jealousy won't stand for it.

"Hey," I say, and I pull her to me.

"What?" she murmurs, trying to play it off.

Like I don't know the shot glass comment got her thinking about some hard times.

Baby Girl has big feelings and I know thinking about those years of running brings up bad memories for her.

I hug her to me. This is the side I've been dying to know.

The one where she takes off the mask. The one where she lets me in.

Maria sighs and wraps her arms around my waist, putting her head on my chest.

Fuck.

This woman feels so good in my arms. I can't believe she's finally mine.

The idea that some asshole has been hassling her, threatening her, makes me feel fucking feral.

I've been digging into Matteo Sanchez. That slimy motherfucker has a certain reputation with women.

He's, shall we say, unorthodox in his sexual preferences. Degradation and humiliation are how he gets off.

There've been rumors of missing women. Pros who get paid to do the fucked up shit their clients want.

Now, it's not my business how someone gets off or how someone else makes a living. But if those women are dead somewhere because of this vile fuck, then that is just another reason for me to end his sorry existence.

I kiss Maria's head.

My cock twitches eagerly behind my sweatpants.

She lifts her face.

I know she thinks I am angry over her lying to me, to us, for months. But I'm not. She did what she had to in order to survive.

She's so fucking brave. So strong. And I'm proud of her.

But I'm not one to give out compliments. Instead, I show her.

I wrap my hand around her throat, and I tilt her head back as I fuse my mouth to hers.

She moans and I swallow it down greedily.

My blood boils. I feel my cock thud against my sweats. It's already hard as the titanium rods piercing it.

I know Maria likes my jewelry.

She always seems to find a way to touch my piercings be they on my face, my ears, or my dick.

I can't say I hate it.

In fact, it drives me crazy.

Like now, as I drive my tongue down her throat, her fingers dance over the hoops on both my ears.

She's fucking perfect.

I hoist her up by the ass, and she wraps her legs around me.

"Luc," she moans when I let her up for air.

She kisses my cheeks, my neck, my earlobes, licking and sucking on my hoops, driving me out of my fucking mind.

She wiggles her ass. And her shorts do nothing to stop me from feeling her heated pussy pressing against my abdomen.

Shit.

I falter a step, but I won't fall. I can't.

I'm holding precious fucking cargo.

We make it to the bedroom and I'm tearing at her clothes.

"Luc, need you," she arches her back as I free her glorious tits.

"I got you, Baby Girl," I grunt and follow her onto the bed.

I squeeze her soft flesh, loving how her tits fit perfectly in my hands.

I have pretty big hands with long fingers, and Maria's breasts fit them perfectly.

I memorize the way her bronze skin looks against my paler, tattooed hand and it turns me on so fucking much. I flex my hips, pressing my covered dick against her weeping slit.

Her arousal is soaking the fabric, and I swear to fucking God, I'm going to come if I keep dry humping her.

I move down, and she moans at the loss.

Grinning, I drop biting kisses along her neck, till I reach her cherry ripe nipples.

Who says you can't have dessert before dinner?

"Fuck, Maria, you got my pants all wet," I tell her, standing up and leaving her panting.

"Where are you going?" she asks, and I bite my lip to stop from smiling as I lay down next to her.

"Right here. Now get on your knees, and climb on, Baby Girl."

She licks her lips and starts to straddle my thighs.

"Nuh uh, up here," I say and slap my shoulder.

"W-what?"

"Climb on," I repeat. "Don't make me tell you again."

"But I don't know what—"

"Get that sweet ass over here, Maria, and ride my fucking face."

CHAPTER THIRTY-MARIA

Holy. Sex. God.

Okay, so I'm a big girl. And obviously, before Luc, I was a virgin.

He is the sexiest man I have ever known. And I am so in love with him.

But when he asks me to ride his face, I admit, I freeze.

He's shirtless, wearing only gray sweatpants, which should be fucking outlawed, and Poison is still playing in the background.

I must have hit repeat by accident, but it is low enough it doesn't faze me.

"Climb on," he repeats. *"Don't make me tell you again."*

"But I don't know what—"

"Get that sweet ass over here, Maria, and ride my fucking face."

Luc doesn't wait after barking that last order. I'm sitting on his hips, frozen, and he reaches down and grabs me by the thighs.

Then he just pulls me up his body.

"Oh my God!" I yell as he lifts me.

I don't know how he does it. Like he has stupid strength or something. Anyway, he is always just picking me up like I weigh nothing.

This time, he sets me down with my knees on either side of his head.

"I'll crush you," I mutter, but I can't really think.

Luc has his tongue in my cunt, and his hands gripping my ass, with his nose pressed right against my clit.

"Fuck. You're soaked for me," he growls. "So fucking hot and wet."

Then he is back to lapping at me from my slick entrance to my tiny little nub that is begging for attention. And then I feel it.

"Your tongue is pierced, too?" I ask, and I swear the fucker laughs.

He must have had it out while we were together because this is the first time I feel metal there.

And it feels great.

I don't know how I missed it when he kissed me before. But yeah, I sort of did.

His kisses are always intense, but before he was just driving that talented tongue down my throat and all I could feel was full.

So full.

He completes me in ways I didn't know I needed. And he fucks me like he was born to do it.

God, I love him so much.

Luc licks me just right, circling my clit with the metal ball at the top of his tongue.

He tugs on my hips, and I start to move, following his silent direction while he eats me like a man who's been starving for weeks.

He fucks me with his mouth like he's desperate for me and I have never felt more desired.

I pull his hair, moaning as I start to come.

My orgasm slams into me and I am hardly aware as he flips me over, shoves his pants down, and fills me with his beautiful dick.

He laces our fingers together, his silver eyes burning into mine, and he starts to move.

"Fuck. Baby Girl. So tight. So wet," he groans, then he kisses me.

His eyes are open and so are mine. I don't want to miss a single moment of our coming together.

I know I am new to this. To sex. But every time with Luc, it just gets better.

My heart is thumping so loudly I wonder if he can hear it.

"That's it. Let me in. Fuck. Christ."

He is on his knees now, and he's pulled me with him, so my ass is resting on his thighs as he drives into me, pounding into my needy pussy.

"Not close enough," he growls, then he withdraws and flips me onto my belly.

Luc lifts my hips, I'm still trying to catch my breath, but I can't.

He slams into me from behind, then wraps one hand around my throat and the other around my waist as he lifts me up, so I am mimicking his stance.

"Luc!" I shout, feeling him so deep, I swear he must be hitting my goddamn soul.

"That's it. Scream for me," he says.

And as the most explosive orgasm I have ever felt sends me tumbling into oblivion, I do.

I scream.

"LUC!"

Eons later, I blink my eyes and realize I must have passed out. Luc is missing from the bed, but he's draped a sheet over my body, and I smile.

He is so careful with me.

The central air conditioner is turned up, and it is blasting through the vents. I am chilly without his big body surrounding me, so I snuggle into the sheet.

I know I should get up, but I don't want to. My body feels deliciously sore, and I'm still caught somewhere between dream and reality.

I like it there. I enjoy being in that place where I have no responsibilities, no fears or doubts, only soft feelings.

Luc always seemed so quiet. He did not look like the kind of man to give commands, but in the bedroom, he does.

And I never thought I could be the type of woman to follow them. But I do. And I like it.

Something about handing him control feels so good. It feels right. And I hope it goes on forever.

I grin as I hear footsteps coming towards the bedroom. It's Luc, and he's humming.

Every Rose Has Its Thorn.

Of course, he is humming that song. It must have played for an hour.

"Hey, Baby Girl," he says, walking towards me with a plate and a fork.

He is deliciously naked. While I am busy staring

at his chiseled, inked up, and beautifully pierced body, my stomach growls.

"Brought you something," he says, grinning at me and I slide over so he can sit.

I glance down at the plate and smile. It is full of fresh berries and whipped cream and little pieces of angel food cake.

"Mmmm. But you only brought one fork."

I point out, nodding to the plate.

"Aren't you going to share?"

"Yeah, Baby Girl, I'm gonna share, but everything that goes in your mouth when you're lying in this bed, I'm gonna be the one to put it there."

It's such a pigheaded, over the top thing to say.

And like everything with this man, I fucking love it.

"Open wide," he commands, and I listen.

"Mmmm. That is so good," I say after I take a raspberry dipped in cream from his fork.

"Wider," he says this time, and feeds me a piece of cake.

Soon, Luc drops the fork on the floor. He's feeding me by hand. Then, with his mouth.

And I eat it. I take everything he offers.

Sucking down berries along with his pierced

tongue and moaning when he rubs whipped cream between my legs and laps it all off.

By the time I'm on my knees, taking his cock as far as it will go down my throat, we've eaten everything and made a mess while doing it.

And when I'm swallowing his hot, sweet cum, watching Luc's face as he gives himself over to the pleasure I bring him, I realize it is worth it.

Everything I have ever been through is so fucking worth it to have this time with him.

I love him.

CHAPTER THIRTY-ONE-MARIA

It's been a couple of weeks since I moved into Luc's home, and it's been, *it's been magic.*

Every day Luc shows me another facet of himself, and when I put it with all the rest of the things I know about him, I can't imagine how this brilliant, beautiful, amazing man isn't taken already.

Well, he is taken now.

This one is mine, ladies.

Sorry, not sorry.

I haven't been back to work at the Den, and at first, I didn't really notice. I mean, when a girl is being wined and dined by one of the most powerful men in the city, it's pretty hard to pay attention to anything else.

And I don't get it.

He has me already.

Body, heart, and soul.

Every day, I tell him I love him.

He doesn't say it back. And that's okay.

Love shouldn't be greedy.

That's what I tell my desperate heart every time I start to doubt whether he ever will.

Every night, I show him how I feel with my body. I submit to his will. I give him everything. And I let him teach me how to love him.

I think I satisfy him. I mean, I hope I do.

The way he can't seem to stop touching me and kissing me. The sounds he makes when he sinks into my wet heat.

All this tells me he cares. That he's in this thing, too.

It hits me right then.

For the first time in my life, I'm happy.

Genuinely happy.

And it is all because of him.

I pinch myself as I ride in the elevator with Giselle.

Yeah, sometimes I do feel like it's all a dream. But then I open my eyes and I see his handsome face, his metal piercings sparkling in the sun, that steel gaze zeroed in on me, and I feel alive.

I must be awake. Because even with all the books I've been reading, courtesy of our magnificent home library, I just don't think I could dream up a man like him.

Everything he feels is written all over his face. Knowing that warms me.

Luc might be careful with his words, but that look he gives me, you know the one.

The one that makes jet fighters zoom around inside my stomach.

The one that makes my heart beat double time.

And my pussy clench with need.

Yeah, that look.

Well, that look says he is really into me. And that's good enough.

He's perfect.

He's mine.

Luc is everything I have ever wanted and so much more.

I don't need the words. I just need him.

"Hey, how is your mother? Have you seen her lately?" Giselle asks.

"Oh, Mami's hospital bed was just delivered. She just got out a couple of days ago. Her neighbor is staying with her for a few days until her strength returns. Honestly, I think there is something going on there. Oh, and Luc hired a cleaning service, too. But I visited her every day at the hospital with him."

Sisi looks surprised, but I'm not. No matter what he is doing or how busy he is, I know he's always there for me.

Except for now, of course. I can't say I love him being away from home. But he texts me every couple of hours to check in. And that settles my anxious nerves.

Mami is at her best around noon. I hate to bother her when she is resting, so that is the time we usually go to visit.

The doctor's prognosis is highly favorable. They are talking full recovery, and I am just beside myself with joy.

Joe is usually there, and I am starting to wonder if there is maybe something more to their friendship.

I mean, I hope there is.

He is such a good man, and Mami deserves to be happy.

Anna is on bedrest, and I've been visiting her with Giselle a lot. She's so brave and I admire the relationship she has with Nico.

How a sweet woman like her wound up with a

scary dude like him, I will never know. But I guess Nico has his good points.

He's been a good boss, and now that I am living with Luc, he attempts to be more approachable. I think he's even smiled at me once or twice.

It's kind of scary. But for Anna's sake, I keep that to myself.

And I get it. I did kind of look desperate for a while there, but I was desperate.

I'm so glad Luc has forgiven me for that.

I miss him.

He understands why I set my cap at the king of the Vipers. I'm embarrassed by it, but it is what it is.

I can own my mistakes.

Still, I hope Luc knows there was never anything there.

No feelings.

No attraction.

I just wanted to see my mother, to be able to come home without hiding or being afraid.

As it turns out, I don't need the king for that.

I need the council. I need Luc. He's the one man task force dedicated to increasing the power, money, and holdings of the Vipers and Viper Enterprises.

But really, I don't care about what he does. He could be a pauper and I would still love him.

I just need Luc. And I'll take him in any way, shape, or form.

Giselle sighs, and I turn my head to look at her.

I know she has this thing with Angel.

I mean, I don't know what it is exactly, but it is something. And I wonder if she is okay.

"You finally working tonight?" she asks as the elevator doors open.

I shake my head. I haven't discussed this with the girls yet. I'm not really sure if it's their business, to be honest.

"Nah. Actually, I am going to have a lot more free time now that the guys are away."

"Oh, why's that?" she asks as the armed guard looks at our IDs, as if he doesn't know who we are, and lets us in.

"Well, apparently, I am not allowed to work anymore. Especially not while Luc is out of town," I tell her.

"What? Maria, that is ridiculous!"

She is outraged. But all I want to do is smile.

"Really, it's not like that. He's just being protective and supportive. Truth is, I want to go back to school," I tell her, then motion for her to zip our lips.

We already agreed Anna didn't need any stress during her last month of pregnancy.

So, no talking about my problems.

And yeah, I do have problems, despite being deliriously happy, living with the man of my dreams.

Mami was released from the hospital the day before he left for Boston with Nico and Angel.

Luc was in an emergency meeting with Nico when she called me with the news, and I needed to go.

I didn't want to interrupt. But I can't go without telling him.

I think about that day for the last few seconds of the elevator ride.

A *few days ago*
Mami just called, and I am so happy. She is getting out!

I text Luc.

> ME
>
> I am so sorry to interrupt, Luc, Mami is being released. I'm going to grab a ride share and pick her up.

LUC

No. I'm assigning half a dozen armed bodyguards to accompany you. They will take you to pick your mother up.

ME

6? Don't you think that's overkill?

I wait, but he doesn't reply. And a second later, a driver knocks on the door and there are two SUVs with armed guards.

Turned out, it wasn't overkill.

Mami thought it was hilarious, having all those big muscle men escorting us around.

But when we get her home, there is an unexpected visitor on the porch, and I'm glad those guys are with us.

And that they have guns.

I recognize the miserable jerk immediately. Even though the years have not been kind, it is pretty hard to mistake him for anyone else.

Matteo Sanchez is standing on my mother's porch there in all his greasy-haired glory.

I remain in the car. Yes, I'm supposed to follow her inside, but the second I see him I freeze.

"Stay here, *mija*," Mami says.

The driver gets out to escort her and Mami just plays it off like nothing is amiss.

Right on cue, Joe, the neighbor who's been helping her, walks over from where he is weeding his yard.

I can't hear anything they say, but Joe is clever.

He has his phone in his hand.

I think he is recording. But no.

Smart guy.

Joe calls Luc, and he leaves the line open for him to hear everything that goes on between Matteo and my mother.

I don't know that yet.

Not until I arrive at the Den. I'm supposed to meet Luc inside.

But when we pull into the back, I see him outside, waiting for me.

He looks mad as hell.

I shouldn't get turned on by that. But seeing Luc in a temper is a sight to behold.

His piercings glitter like his eyes, and he looks like something from out of this world.

Dark gray pants cling to his hips and thighs, and I imagine the serpentine tattoo that winds around his body, ending with his long, thick, jewelry covered cock.

I swear I swoon at the thought.

He looks like something out of that Gerard Butler movie. The ancient warrior one.

300.

That's what it's called. The one about the Spartans.

He dazzles me.

Beneath his clothes, I know he looks even better.

Tattooed and dripping metal. I picture the Spartans in that film. Then I picture the sexy as fuck bad guy.

Xerxes.

In the movie, Xerxes is dripping gold, and Luc is like the counter version.

His metal is silver-colored titanium.

My pussy aches for him and I can't stop my mind from picturing him.

All that tanned skin covering his long, muscled up body. His ink is superb and the way he compliments it with sexy as fuck piercings.

Shit.

Luc is a dream. An erotic, hypnotic dream of a man.

And he is all mine.

My mouth is watering for him.

"Hey—" I start, but he's already moving towards me.

He doesn't give me a chance to speak, he just grabs me to him in a tight hug.

His body is so hard and warm from standing in the summer afternoon heat. But he's vibrating with emotion.

I'm confused. And a little worried. I hum deep in my throat, clinging to him, trying to soothe him.

I breathe him in, loving the spicy scent of his body wash.

He pulls back and cups my cheeks, claiming my mouth in one of his deliciously possessive kisses.

Then, he tells me what happened.

After he's finished telling me the veiled threats Matteo made to my mother about me, Luc tells me something else.

He tells me he has to leave for a little while and my heart stutters inside my chest.

"Listen to me," he begins.

"I told Nico about your connection to Sanchez."

I freeze.

Oh, my God.

What must the king of the Vipers think about that?

"D-does he want me to leave town?"

"What? No! You are not going anywhere, Baby Girl," he says, and I expel a sharp breath.

I don't know why I panic. I guess I just figure Nico might not believe I have nothing to do with the Sanchez brothers or their sudden interest in fucking with the Vipers.

"Listen, Maria, you are mine. Hear me? You are staying with me. Now look, I am sorry, but I have to go away for a few days on business with the guys," he says.

"Where? For how long?" I ask, and I grip his shirt in my hands.

I don't even realize I am doing it until I feel his hands closing over mine. He kisses my head again, his steel eyes softening.

"Just for a few days. We have a business meeting in Boston. But that's not important," he continues. "What is important is I won't be here, and I need you safe. You will do what I say, won't you?"

Of course, I agree.

"I can't have anything happen to you, Baby Girl."

"I need you safe, too. I'll be fine," I tell him.

I just didn't know then how bored I would be.

CHAPTER THIRTY-TWO-LUC

I stand next to Angel in the hall as Nico has his meeting with Liam O'Doyle and his twenty year old daughter Margaret.

The old man has her pimped out in some trashy get up like she's up for grabs and I feel nothing but revulsion.

What the fuck is wrong with him that he would blatantly offer his daughter like some carnal sacrifice?

It makes me sick.

I don't often accompany Nico to these kinds of meetings. Not unless there is something legal to be discussed. But the O'Doyle's are old school Irish mob, and they have something we want.

I'm not there to negotiate terms. I am there to pick up on something they might be hiding.

And I can see it as soon as I look at the old man's wrinkled maw.

This motherfucker has Sanchez Junior.

And we want him.

But I want his brother more.

Ever since I heard Matteo Sanchez's slimy, high-pitched voice asking Maria's frail mother if she's heard from her daughter, my hackles have been raised.

"You see your daughter lately, Senora Lopez? You know, she broke my heart that Mia. Yours too, si? Don't worry, Mami. We will see her again. Soon."

Every inch of me is on high alert. And I hate that I am here.

I fucking loathe that I left her home.

Maria is mine.

She's become so damn important to me.

I know I have what some might regard as an unhealthy obsession, but I really don't care.

She is essential to me. A necessary part of my life.

I need her more than I need air, or food, or water.

Maria is my sustenance.

She nourishes me with her love that she gives so freely. With her body that I find so divine. With her mind, that is brilliant and funny. And with her sweet smiles, and the way she naturally gravitates to and attracts all things joyful.

I think about the way she gave her virginity to me, and I rub the hollow part of my chest.

I recall how good she tastes on my lips, and I lick them, hoping to find a remnant of her there.

Fuck.

I wish I was back home with her.

Then I pause because I realize Maria has made my renovated warehouse a real home.

Sure, it was already set up. A little snooty for the area I grew up, but there was a lot of real estate development on the Hudson now.

But with her brightly colored pillows and her eclectic tastes in food, music, and art, she's turned my cold, minimalist place into something warm and vibrant.

Fuck, I love her.

I've known it for a while now.

I haven't said the words yet. But I should. I need to.

Maria is so damn pure and innocent. But she's not just some goody two shoes.

She's got a penchant for mischief. And it makes her irresistible.

My devious little minx.

I know I am not good.

I've done bad things.

Terrible things.

Things that some people would never dream of doing.

All that stuff started before I got my law degree. Some of it when I wasn't even legal yet.

But with my education, I achieved a new understanding about life and the roles we take on.

I think Maria understands it, too.

She likes philosophy. I catch her reading a lot in the library, and it melts something inside of me.

She likes Dante, and when I tell her I have an old copy of *The Divine Comedy* in the original vernacular Italian, she begs to see it.

I show her, and we discuss religion and politics. Then I read from it, and she goes wild.

Apparently, Maria has a thing for guys who read and speak Italian.

Lucky for me, I do. And I wonder how she'll react when she learns I speak Spanish, Greek, and a little Russian, too.

She is so fucking hot.

But philosophy is a tricky thing. It makes me think, and I'm the kind of man to get lost in thought.

Good.

Bad.

Which am I?

Am I good or bad for her?

Do I taint her with the bad things I've done?

I push that last thought far out of my brain. Maria might be good, too good truth be told.

But she's lied. She's kept secrets. She is multifaceted, like any precious gem should be.

Besides, I don't care about all that. All I care about is that she is mine.

The things I am party to are not all legal, but I have my own ideas of right and wrong. I'm a monster sometimes.

A snake.

But I am her monster, and that makes all the difference.

I try to keep the viper inside me tightly coiled. It's the only way he doesn't take over.

But lately, he's been slithering to the surface.

The beast in me knows when someone threatens what's mine.

And someone has been threatening my Maria.

If I let him out, if I unleash the beast and all his vengeance, I will become a thing of pure fucking rage.

If she sees it, will she shy away?

I don't want to scare her, but I need to protect her. To cherish her.

Life isn't black and white. It's gray.

I'm not talking fifty shades. I'm talking mother-fucking thousands.

It's a tricky thing trying to say what is good and what is bad.

You can't label everything. No matter how hard you try.

I'm bad. But what I feel for Maria? That's good.

There is no black and white.

Only gray. Hundreds of thousands of different shades of gray.

How dark you go all depends on the circumstances. Mine are pretty extenuating.

All the shit I've done.

All the tragedy I've seen.

My father leaving.

My sister overdosing in a dirty alley.

My mother slipping into alcoholism.

Her dealer skipping bail.

City politicians not giving a fuck.

Criminals running parks and schools.

After all the years of fighting and clawing my way up through all the shit and shitty people, now I am one of the ones in power.

The Vipers are more than a criminal syndicate. We are a family.

And family is power.

That's something Nico identified back when we were kids, after my sister and his mother died from dirty drugs.

He knew we were better together. Stronger, too.

We slithered and crawled our way to the top. With Angel training us, backing us up, there was no stopping us then.

Just like there is no stopping us now.

O'Doyle might think he has the upper hand, hiding our enemy. But we will find him. We always do.

I'm taking notes on my cell, listening when O'Doyle's men mention thinks like "the package" and "the prize".

These assholes have no idea who they're dealing with.

A few weeks ago, I watched a video of Nico Fury gauging out some asshole's eyes for peeping on his wife.

What does this moron O'Doyle think is going to happen when I confirm Nico's suspicion that he's hiding the guy who threatened Nico's pregnant wife?

Yeah.

It's not something good, I can tell you that.

And I'm about two seconds from confirming it. I have dozens of people working for me. For the Vipers.

Hundreds, even.

When I think about Maria, I understand Nico's actions a little better.

There is something about the curvy little seductress that disintegrates any shred of civilization left in my moral compass.

Hell.

The damn thing might be broken for all I know.

Angel's phone pings, and he grunts, trying to take it out of his tight fucking jeans.

Not his fault, really. He's just built like a Mack truck.

It's been twenty minutes, and I'm getting impatient.

I should be home. With her.

An image of Matteo Sanchez flits through my mind, and I get mad.

That asshole seems to have an unhealthy attachment to my woman. And I am just the man to relieve him of that disturbing fucking delusion.

I will too. As soon as I get back home.

I should text her.

And I'm about to, but Angel finally gets his phone open.

"Oh fuck," he grunts, and then I see Nico running towards us.

CHAPTER THIRTY-THREE-MARIA

"You're gonna be okay, sweetheart," I coo to Anna who is sobbing uncontrollably in her hospital bed.

It was late when Giselle called me with Anna on the line. The latter was hysterical. She started spotting and was worried about the baby, so I told her to call an ambulance.

Luckily, we got there as they arrived, and Sisi and I both bullied our way into the vehicle.

Not like the EMTs were going to say no when there were six armed bodyguards with us.

In fact, one joined us in the back of the ambulance.

"Why the hell is it hot in here? I'm going to get a nurse," Giselle says.

Luc texts me every fifteen minutes with an update and I am so relieved every time he does.

It's been a week, and time has been crawling. But excitement fills me at the prospect of having him home.

"I can't believe I made a big deal out of nothing," Anna says, hiccuping from her crying bout.

"Don't be silly, Anna. It could have been a very big deal. I'm just so thankful it's not, and you and the baby are safe," I tell her, and she tries to smile, but it's wobbly.

"There! They fixed the AC," Giselle says coming back with a cup of ice water for Anna.

"Thank you, guys. You're the best," she replies and drinks from the straw.

After a little while, I hear some commotion, and I look to see Nico Fury bearing down towards us, and he looks like a whirlwind.

He ignores us, going straight for his wife, and that is fine. Because I just want to see Luc.

I don't have to wait long.

The piercing on his eyebrow glitters as he turns the corner and enters the hall leading to Anna's private room, and I don't wait.

I take off. I run to him, and my heart practically

leaps with joy when he catches me and holds me tight.

"Fuck, that feels good. I am not leaving you home ever again, Baby Girl," he says, groaning as he kisses me. "Next time, you are coming with me."

It's not an *I love you*, but it makes me wild for him.

CHAPTER THIRTY-FOUR-LUC

I've had Maria in my bed for the past ten hours, and I don't think we've slept for more than two.

If I'm not kissing her, I'm touching her. I can't seem to stop.

I run my hands over every dip and curve, memorizing her as if I could ever forget.

I spend a lot of time tasting the freckles that dance across her nose and tracing the pair of dimples she has at the bottom of her spine, right above her sweet peach of an ass.

I sip from her lips, then I move to her cheek, her chin, her neck.

I bite her there, where her neck meets her shoulder, and she yelps.

And no matter what I do, I can't stop myself from

sliding my dick into her tight, wet cunt again and again. And again.

Fuck. Me.

But *don't ever stop fucking me* is what I really mean.

I'm insatiable.

So hungry for this woman. I want to consume her.

I fuck her relentlessly. Pounding into her cunt, and she takes it.

Hell, she is greedy for it.

I love the fact that I am the only man who's ever been inside her slick wet heat.

"And you're the only man who ever will," she whimpers, and I realize I am so far gone I am talking out loud.

"That's right, Baby Girl. This is my pussy. Tell me."

I'm on tenterhooks waiting for her to tell me what I already know.

This woman was made for me. I own her.

Just like she owns me. And it feels so good to admit that, even if only to myself. I'll tell her, too.

One day.

I watch as her eyes glaze over, and she parts her kiss stung lips.

"Yours, Luc. All yours."

Dark, scary thoughts fill my head at the thought of anyone else even looking at her with intent.

Maria is right. She's all mine.

"That's it, Baby. Keep going."

I lay back, enjoying the view of my woman riding my dick.

She is so, *so thick.*

I love how she feels. I can't get enough of touching her.

So curvy.

So soft.

She's got all this smooth bronze skin, and in the dim light it glitters like gold. I want to pierce her.

Maybe her nipples. Or that pretty little clit.

Fuck, my balls squeeze just imagining it. Of course, I'd be the one to do it. No one else sees my girl naked.

Not unless they have a death wish.

Her big thighs squeeze my hips, and I groan, sitting up so I can touch more of her.

"Close, Luc," she tells me.

My Baby Girl is, she's *vocal.*

She tells me everything she feels.

How full my cock feels, stretching her tight cunt.

The way my piercings roll and stroke deep inside her.

How much she likes it when I whisper filthy things to her.

"That's it, Baby. Keep fucking me till you get off. Let me watch you come," I tell her, and I grab onto her ass.

Fuck, her ass is perfection. Her softness welcomes me. I knead it as I suck her nipple into my mouth.

Definitely getting her a nipple ring, I tell myself.

Maria is a thing of pure beauty.

Like a goddess, come to earth just for me to worship.

And I do.

Fuck, yes, I do.

"You're so hungry for my dick, aren't you? Tell me again whose pussy this is," I demand as I keep squeezing her sweet ass, teasing her forbidden hole with my pinky.

I want to fuck her there.

Soon.

I want my cum leaking out of every hole. Every inch of her needs to be mine.

"Always, Luc. I always want you. Yours. My pussy

is all yours," she moans the words and lifts her hands up to her hair.

It's wild now. No more color depositing shampoo or conditioner. It's a million shades of brown and gold and red, and it is fantastic.

Just like every inch of her.

My dick throbs, my balls tighten.

I feel every barbell roll as she slides up and down, gripping my cock with her snug channel.

Maria rocks her hips faster, chasing her orgasm.

And I am a goner.

She grunts and drops her hands to my chest. Her almond eyes are lust glazed and so fucking sexy.

"Luc, I'm gonna," she moans.

I am so fucking lucky.

This woman is all mine. She sees all of me. Every dark shadow and blood-stained inch. And she loves it.

She loves *me.*

And *I* love *her.*

Just as she comes, I flip her onto her back. I pin her hands above her head, and I pound into her.

Her cunt tightens, and her eyes are wide as she moans long and loud.

"Luuuc!"

I should be gentler. I should be sweet with her. She's new to this. To sex. To me.

I shouldn't go so hard.

But I'm not in control anymore. I'm like a fucking animal for her.

My viper is in charge now, and the beast is out to claim his woman.

That creature I keep tightly wound has slithered all the way to the surface.

And he's a possessive bastard.

"Give it to me, Baby Girl. Gimme another," I demand.

"I-I can't."

But we both know that's a lie.

"Give it to me, Maria. That's mine," I tell her.

Her eyes go even wider.

But I know she likes it. Her pussy is still spasming. Her breasts are jiggling. And I can't decide which I like better.

She's struggling against my hands. I know she likes to touch me. But I won't loosen my grip.

Not this time.

I need to control her. To stamp myself all over her.

I need to, to *own her.*

I slam my cock into her, and the sound is so wet.

The slapping of flesh is, well, it's loud.

Her arousal is dripping down to my balls, letting me slide deep, *so fucking deep*.

All of it is just so loud. So filthy. So fucking mine.

I reach between us, and I pinch her clit, and fuck, yes, her pussy squeezes me.

Now, she's coming again.

But this time, she sucks the load right out of my dick with her hot little slit.

I let it happen. I let her give me some of that joy she seems to carry around like extra pocket change.

And I take it all in.

Her sounds.

Her softness.

Her tastes.

The way she takes my pierced cock, and no, I'm not being conceited, but it's big and it's thick, and she fits me like a goddamn glove.

I take it all in and I let her surround me.

I sink into her welcoming flesh. Her pussy spasms, fluttering all around me.

And I join her in erotic bliss, filling her with so much hot cum it trickles down her thighs.

And as I raise my head to watch, my heart squeezes.

Maria is lying there, glistening with sweat, sticky white fluid smearing across her skin.

And she looks more beautiful than ever.

She looks like mine.

There's a long scar slashed across Luc's back. I trace it with light fingers.

I want to ask him how he got it, but I don't want to break the spell we both seem to have fallen under.

The last couple of weeks with him have been sublime.

Every minute, he sinks deeper under my skin.

Into my heart.

Stamping himself on my very soul.

I must have asked him though, because he opens his mouth, and his gravelly voice reaches my ears.

He sounds so sexy as he explains where he got it.

"I told you my sister OD'd when I was a teenager. But I didn't tell you that right before I joined up with Nico and Angel, I tried to go it alone."

"You did?"

"Yeah. So the guys responsible were in this neighborhood gang. Just a bunch of low-level dealers and pushers. Idiots didn't even have a name," he says without emotion.

"I'm sorry about your sister," I whisper.

"Thank you. Anyway, I wanted to shut them down, so I went after them. But I was a stupid kid. I had no backup. And they beat me up, wanted to make sure I remembered the lesson," he explains.

I make a humming sound, wanting him to continue.

"They had me tied up and stuck in some stash house closet. Then the guy in charge, he walks in, and he's cocky as fuck. He has a knife in his hand, his buddies turn me around, hold me down, and he slices me," he says, and I am filled with so much anger.

My heart is breaking for teenaged Luc. I feel tears spill down my cheeks and then he's shifting, turning over so he can cradle me to his warm, hard chest.

"Hey, it's alright. It was a long time ago," he murmurs, kissing my forehead.

"I am just so sorry you had to go through that," I tell him, and I mean it.

"It's okay, Baby Girl. If I didn't go through that, then I wouldn't be here now. And this is exactly where I want to be," he says.

Luc's eyes blaze silver and eager pleasure fills me.

His long hand wraps around my throat, and he tilts my head, pressing his mouth to mine.

Goddamn, I love it when he kisses me.

There's something to be said for having a man's complete attention, and when Luc kisses me, I know I have his.

And it shifts something inside of me.

I moan, clinging to his wrist as he slides that deliciously pierced tongue in and out of my mouth.

He groans, moving over me, and I feel his hard cock at my entrance.

"You wet for me, Maria?" he asks, and I nod.

I am wet. Fucking soaked.

All he has to do is look at me and my pussy reacts. My entire body lights up like the fourth of July.

Maybe it's desperate. But I don't know how to play coquettish games.

I want Luc. And I want him to know I do.

"Wait," I say, and he pauses immediately.

I love the way Luc bosses me around in bed, but I also love that he listens to me.

"What is it, Baby Girl?"

I peek up at him through my lashes and have to find some confidence before I say it.

"I-I want to try something. Can I?" I ask.

Luc's lips twitch and he nods.

He cocks his head while I sit up.

Like he's more curious than anything, as I tell him to lie back down.

"What are you doing, Baby Girl?" he asks, and his eyes are glittering, so I know he likes it.

"You'll see," I tell him, and I grin like the Cheshire cat.

I might be a novice to this, but now that I have Giselle and Anna to talk to, well, let's just say there are things girls talk about when their men aren't around.

Things about sexy times that are actually quite informative.

Luc's chest rumbles as I slide over his long body, rubbing my skin against his, petting him with my hands, my hair, my tits as I move down until I am between his splayed legs.

I have zero inhibitions when it comes to this man.

But I am nervous about this. I want Luc to like it.

I look at him while I try to wrap as much of one hand as I can around the base of his thick staff.

His cock is fucking beautiful.

I know that sounds weird, but it is.

Long, thick, studded with titanium bars and balls, and that big, thick ring coming from the tip.

Combined with the tattoo winding around his hips, Luc looks like a bonafide sex god.

My very own Xerxes.

Warrior god.

But my Luc will have a better ending.

Hopefully, we both will. Very, very soon.

I moan as I drop plucking kisses along his lower abdomen, paying attention to that V that drives me crazy.

Luc stretches and runs his fingers over my head through my hair.

Encouraged, I continue.

When Luc eats me, he makes me feel like I'm delicious. Like I am better than chocolate or whiskey or both.

He makes me feel cherished, coveted. As if I am the only woman in the world.

I want to treat him to the same.

Not that I want to make him feel like a woman. I

just want him to feel like the only man in the whole universe. Because to me, that is exactly what he is.

So, I slide lower. I run my fingers and lips across his skin, tracing tattoos and loving him with every inch of my soul.

My mouth is watering.

I moan as I lick him from his puckered hole to his heavy sack and further still until I swallow the pearl of precum at the tip of his cock.

I do it again, and again. I get bolder, I tongue fuck his ass, teasing him with the tip of my pinky while I move to his sack.

My man is very serious about hygiene. He is trimmed and cleaned, moisturized, and inked to fucking perfection. Like a mouthwatering dream.

I'm crazy for him. I want to do everything to make him feel good. Anything at all.

I push in a little bit.

"Fuck," he hisses, arching his back.

I follow his lead. Doing only what he seems to like, and now, I am tracing his barbells and hoops with my tongue, tugging on them, and licking his shaft as I go.

Goddamn, he is so fucking sexy.

Luc talks to me. He tells me I'm his Good Girl, shows me what he likes.

And the thing is, I like it, too.

His thighs are wide, and I love the way his body feels surrounding me. His hands are on my head. He's flexing his hips, and I take him as deep as I can.

I knew this would be hot, but I did not know it would turn me on so much.

My pussy is aching, begging for attention. I am fucking soaked.

But Luc he tastes so good. Fucking divine. And I can't stop.

I lick him, lapping at his flesh again and again, jerking his shaft as I do.

I roll my tongue over his Jacob's ladder. I suck on the piercing circling his tip.

I want to give him everything.

I do give him everything.

Using my body, I show him how much I love him.

I use my lips, my mouth, even my teeth as I fondle and stroke my man.

"Fuck, Baby Girl, I'm gonna cum," he says, like it's a warning.

But it's what I want.

He's up on his elbows, watching me, and fuck, I can't wait for him to fill my mouth.

I close my lips over his head, jerking him with

one hand while I continue to tease his asshole with my other.

Luc grabs my head, holds it while he flexes his hips and I gag as the ball on the tip of his cock ring hits the back of my throat.

I turn my head a little sideways, so he can go deeper. And he does.

I feel so empowered. Sexy, too, as my man fucks my throat. My pussy is dripping down my thighs.

He's just so fucking hot.

Then Luc flexes hard, and he is roaring my name. Next, I'm swallowing him down. As much of it as I can.

Some spills down my chin, but still, I smile when I lift my head, swiping up the rest and sticking my finger in my mouth.

"Goddamn, Baby Girl. You look good with my cum dripping down your neck," he growls.

"Let's see how you look with it spilling out of your hot little cunt."

"Yes, please," I reply.

And I swap places with him, burying my fingers in his curly hair as he licks into my pussy with his long, snake-like tongue.

"I love you, Luc," I cry out as my first orgasm washes over me.

"Hold on to the headboard," he says, and I moan.

"Gonna fuck you till you see stars," he promises.

I believe him.

Because my man delivers.

And he does. He makes me see stars.

This time, and the next time, too.

CHAPTER THIRTY-SIX-LUC

Work has been busy as we hunt down that motherfucker.

Sanchez.

Of course, I want the other one. The brother.

Matteo.

But I haven't told anyone about that yet. Nico has other things to worry about and Angel, well, he's been preoccupied with his own shit.

Nico is talking and I should be listening, but all my thoughts are on my woman.

Who knew my Maria would turn into such a dirty little girl after I took her virginity?

Truth is, she is as insatiable for me as I am for her, and it makes me hard as fuck just thinking about it.

Remembering the way her mouth felt as she kissed me from my asshole to cockhole, and how her tight cunt strangled my dick when she came, Twice.

I almost pop a boner right there.

Then I see Nico staring at me, and I clear my throat.

"We've heard from Callahan. He says fuck O'Doyle, his loyalty is ours," I tell him.

"That's because his next shipment is stuck on our fucking docks," Angel inserts.

He isn't wrong.

"Good. At least he knows who has the power," Nico says. "And maybe he'll spread the news. Let him know, the minute I have Sanchez, the Vipers will reopen everything."

"You got it, Boss," I tell Nico.

He's checking his watch, and I know he wants to get back to the hospital.

Anna delivered their baby boy three weeks early, but he's healthy as a horse and the little mama is doing good.

In fact, I'm going to follow him there in my car.

I dropped Maria off before coming here so she could visit with Anna while I get some work done.

Angel is saying something about new protocols

regarding our security and I'm only half listening as I send a text to Maria.

ME

I'll be there in forty-five minutes.

BABY GIRL

Okay. I miss you.

ME

Already?

BABY GIRL

I am always missing you. Always wanting you, Luc. You know that.

ME

Good. I'll see you soon.

BAEY GIRL

Can't wait. I love you.

I grunt and I stare at her last message.

My chest squeezes. There is a tightness there I have never felt before. It isn't comfortable.

In fact, it kind of hurts.

But I know what it is. It's like that character from that fucking kid's movie.

The one with furry green fucker whose heart is shriveled right up until the end of the Christmas story.

But the ending is the thing. That is when his heart grows. It gets bigger. So big, it breaks the fucking thing measuring it.

Maria loves me. I know she does. And knowing it makes me feel ten feet tall.

I should say it back.

I should tell Maria that I love her simply because I do.

So fucking much.

But I don't. And that has more to do with my hangups than any lack on her part.

Maria doesn't lack for anything.

She is perfect.

Tell her already.

I will, I tell myself.

I will.

"You ready to finish this fucking meeting?" Nico says, and I glance up at him and Angel.

Shit.

"Yeah. So, this is what we know about O'Doyle's connection to Sanchez," I say and give them a rundown on how those two pieces of shit came across one another, running guns and drugs.

The thing is, they both need the Vipers to do it.

But they don't want to pay. And everyone has to pay.

We live in a world of trolls and tolls. Civilization is pretty much grounded in this one system where a person or organization has control over access routes, information, goods, or what have you.

Gatekeepers.

It is all about the gatekeepers.

And if you want what they have, you must pay. Period.

There is no other way.

In this scenario, the Vipers have control of the port.

If O'Doyle and Sanchez want to play there, they need to pay. But if they want war, well, we can do that as well.

Nico has proven a hundred times he'll stoop to whatever level of violence our opponents drop to.

"If that's it," Nico says, standing, and Angel is already out the door.

"One second," I tell him.

I feel guilty for believing my own doubts about Maria. It was only a few weeks ago that I told Nico I wasn't sure if Maria was working for Sanchez or not.

"Listen, about Maria," I begin.

"Yeah, what?"

"She was never working for Sanchez," I tell him.

"And?" he says.

"And? Well, you know she's living with me," I say, not sure how to proceed.

"Yeah? Look, Luc, spit it the fuck out. I wanna go see my woman and kid," he says.

"I just wanted to tell you and to, *shit*, I guess I don't know," I say, rubbing the back of my neck and feeling kind of foolish.

"You are a grown ass man, Luc. You want Maria?"

I nod.

"She want you?"

After that blow job she gave me when she ate my ass and fingered it, I think it is safe to say *fuck yes, she wants me*.

I nod again.

"Then take her. I wish you the best. But I gotta go see my Anna now."

"Thanks, bro. Maria is visiting her and Nico Jr. I'll be right behind you," I tell him, and the king of the Vipers tips his head.

After that, I feel *lighter*.

Everything feels better now.

It was my own weakness that doubted Maria. My own inability to accept that somebody as good, as kind, as open as her could ever love me without ulterior motive.

But she does love me.

I know it in my soul.

I'm going to tell her today.

I feel guilty about doubting her and I'll apologize to her. I have to.

I'll confess it when I get her.

My phone buzzes, but I don't text and drive. I take shortcuts to the Medical Center, but Jersey City is so fucking overcrowded.

It takes sixteen minutes for me to get there, and I pull up right next to Nico's SUV.

We take the elevator together. Both of us are too lost in thoughts of our women to talk.

That's fine with me.

The doors open and I follow the king, nodding at our men guarding the queen of the Vipers' door.

I wait for his nod, and we both go inside Anna's room. She looks happy, if tired.

I smile and nod my respects. But something is wrong. It's off.

"Where's Maria?" I ask when Nico finally lets his wife up for air.

"Huh? Oh, she went to get me some thread. I

thought you were picking her up at the craft store, Luc. She texted you," Anna says.

Dread fills my stomach as I grab my phone and open my text messages.

Baby Girl

Hey, Anna needs some thread so I'm gonna run to the craft store by the hospital. Pick me up here.

My eyes meet Nico's and I know he can see my worry.

He frowns, but I am already moving.

I go to the hallway first and I see the driver/bodyguard who should be watching my Maria walking into the hallway with half a sandwich stuffed in his mouth.

"Where is she?" I demand.

"Huh? With Mrs. Fury," he says, but his eyes are wide, and he knows he fucked up.

"If anything happens to her," I threaten, but I don't finish it.

No words come to mind to describe the world of hurt he's in for should any harm come to her. And I'm too busy running to the elevator to try to think of any.

I frantically push the button. Dialing Maria on my cell as I do.

She doesn't pick up.

"What's going on?" Nico asks, and he's beside me.

"I don't know. Could be nothing. But Maria is gone. Her driver is here, and she's not. She's not answering her phone, Nico."

"Fuck, okay. Let's go."

I am in a state of utter fucking panic. But I shake my head.

"Stay with Anna. I got this. Let Angel know. Have him track my location and send me a team."

"I'll do all that, but I am coming with you. You're my brother," Nico says, and I nod, giving in.

"Could be nothing," I repeat as we climb in the elevator, hoping it is.

Nico says nothing and minutes drag by like hours.

Fuck. Shit.

I picture Maria's smiling face. I can't wait to see it.

We'll talk about how important it is for her to always have a bodyguard with her when I get her home, safe and sound.

She has to be safe.

Maria just has to be.

Please be fucking safe.

CHAPTER THIRTY-SEVEN-MARIA

The hospital room smells like a combination of antiseptic spray and Ivory soap, and I am okay with that.

Anna just fed Nico Jr, and I have to say, that baby is seriously adorable.

"He has such a nice head," I say, and Anna looks at me like I am crazy.

"What?"

"Look, I don't know why, but it's a thing. Mami always says babies with round heads are perfect. Nico Jr. has a nice round head," I say and shrug.

"Girl, you are so weird. But thank you, I guess. How is your mother doing?" Anna asks.

I tell her about the latest round of chemo and how it hit Mami hard. But she doesn't have to worry because Joe has moved himself in, along with a round-the-clock nurse, courtesy of Luc, and a cleaning service for the house.

"Wow. That is great!" Anna enthuses.

"Where's Sisi? Is she coming today?"

"Sisi went to her family's condo in Florida," she tells me, and I frown. "She needed some space and time to think."

I knew Angel and Sisi were having some sort of disagreement, but I didn't know she left town. Anna is quiet for a moment and the baby coos, capturing both of our attention.

"Here we go. He eats like his father already," Anna says, lifting her baby to her breast.

I smile and hand her a soft nursing blanket and Anna whispers her thanks.

"So, when are they letting you out?"

"Oh, get this," she whispers conspiratorially. "They won't let me out until I poop. Can you believe that? Oh, hey, wanna do me a favor?"

"I am not going to shit in your hospital bath-room, Anna," I tell her deadpan and we both bust out laughing.

Nico Jr. lets out a soft cry as Anna's giggles cause him to detach from her breast.

"Sorry, little guy," I apologize for disturbing his

meal.

Anna laughs one more time before helping him latch back on.

"Oh my God, Maria! No, I do not need you to poop for me. But can you maybe run to Craft Mart and get Mrs. Pirillo another spool of blue thread? I memorized the item number. It's 4567. That way, she can finish the last of the curtains and pillows for the baby's room. I would order them, but the only place that has it is the store," she says.

"Of course, yeah, I can do that," I tell her.

I grin and wave goodbye as baby and mama both start to slip off into sleep. Then, I send Luc a text telling him to pick me up a few streets down from the hospital, because I'm going to go to the store to grab some thread for Anna.

He was supposed to get me anyway, and my driver was going to stay and swap details with one of the other bodyguards.

It should be strange, having all these armed men following me around, but it's not.

Well, not to me.

I grew up in a house full of Sanchez's soldiers. They were always in and out, so it's nothing new. Not really.

I look for my driver in the hallway, but he isn't

there. And I already texted Luc, so I head down to the lobby.

Jersey City is hot as fuck in late July, and today it is worse. It's muggy, and the weather report is calling for rain.

It's been a few weeks since we had any real rain, and I bite my lip just thinking about how amazing a thunderstorm must look from the house.

I still can't believe I live with Luc.

It's like everything I ever wanted and more.

I wave my hand in front of my face as I wait for a traffic light, but it does nothing for me.

I wish I had one of those folding paper fans women used to carry.

It's busy outside, despite the soaring temperatures. People are out doing their thing, and I check my GPS for the location of Craft Mart.

I swear, it doesn't matter that I've passed it a million times. I have the worst sense of direction.

Sweat is making my shorts and tank top stick to my skin as I walk down the street, and I am still looking at the maps app, so it's really no wonder I don't notice anything amiss.

By the time I feel a heavy hand press against my hip, and something hard and cold against my side, it's too late.

"Hello, *nena*. I told you I will always find you," says a menacing voice, and I taste bile build in the back of my throat.

I'm shoved into the back of a low slung car. It's painted a bright, metallic teal, and I wonder how this moron goes unnoticed by anyone.

There's a reason the Vipers are who they are, and the Sanchez cartel's power has dwindled.

"You're making a mistake," I try.

Suddenly, pain explodes in my face, and I cry out, clasping my hands to it.

"Shut up, bitch! You belong to me, and when I get you home, I'm gonna remind you of that."

I scoot closer to the door while Matteo starts shouting orders to his driver in barely comprehensible Spanish.

It must be a dialect or something I just can't understand. But then again, my Spanish has always been more a cool thing to know when I'm in a restaurant as opposed to being fluent enough to converse in the language.

My parents were both practical like that. They wanted me to be American, so I was encouraged to use English when I was a kid.

Seems the older I get, the less I remember.

But I'm not worried about my lack of bilingual

abilities. As Matteo snaps and shouts, I am making sure my cell phone is on.

Luc is the smartest man I know. With any luck, he's using the location app to find me right now.

Please be looking for me.

But even if he's not, I won't regret anything we shared. I won't regret getting complacent and comfortable.

Running was no kind of life for me. And I would rather have a few weeks with Luc than none at all.

He's changed my life. Made it better.

I just hope he knows how much I love him.

CHAPTER THIRTY-EIGHT-LUC

Nico is driving, and in my rearview, I see Angel following us in his big, suped up matte black SUV.

"Do you have her location?" Nico asks.

"Yeah, they're headed down West Side Avenue," I growl.

I watch as the little dot that signifies Maria is getting farther and farther away from me and a tidal wave of emotion slams into me.

It is cold and hard. And it's trying to drown me.

It's fear.

I have to work at it, but I finally push it away.

I have no room for fear. No room for error.

I close my eyes and I exhale.

Fear can't help Maria now. She needs me to be strong.

And what stronger force is there on this earth besides love?

"We'll get her," Nico says.

"I know we will. We have to. I love her," I say it for the first time out loud.

It's not enough. She needs to be the one to hear it. But it is a start.

And it frees me

"They stopped," I practically shout.

I run off the address to Nico, and he adjusts our course.

"We don't tell Anna any of this. She has enough to deal with."

I nod. Anna is his wife, and he can ask anything he wants of me where she is concerned.

My blood is roaring in my ears. I feel the need for violence well inside of me and it's like welcoming an old friend.

Matteo has no fucking idea what he's brought down on him and his whole family.

Business is one thing.

It's like a game of logic and chance and whoever has the biggest balls, the most money and power wins.

But he came for my woman. My Maria. And that makes this personal.

This is about attacking the Vipers. Our family. Our loved ones.

That's a big fucking no-no.

"Angel is calling everyone in. We're convening at the location," Nico says.

"We're gonna get her back, Luc," he adds, and I nod.

The Vipers are moving as one. We're getting into position to ambush our prey.

I feel rage pumping through my veins. Some people say it's poison, but now it's not.

It's fuel. It is exactly what I need to get through this.

I focus. I make a list of who I am and what Matteo Sanchez did.

I am Luc Batiste.

Lawyer.

Businessman.

Tycoon.

I am the Council for the motherfucking Vipers.

And this piece of shit took what's mine.

Now, I'm out for blood.

He attacked me on my turf. On our turf.

The Vipers are an organization that thrives on loyalty.

When one is under siege, we all feel the insult. And we all deliver the punishment together.

It's been a while since we acted. Since we hit back inside the city limits. Hard and out in the open.

Matteo Sanchez fucked with the wrong woman.

I will get my Baby Girl back and when I do, I will make sure everyone knows just how fucking impermissible it is for anyone to fuck with my woman. With any of our women.

Our kingdom might be forged on lies. But there is one truth in all of this. There is one thing that no one can refute.

It's the one thing circling my brain.

One absolute certainty. And it goes for everybody.

You fuck with a Viper, you get bit. And no one walks away from that.

Matteo Sanchez is about to be wiped from the face of the planet. How he goes will depend on what I find.

He better fucking pray I find her whole.

Unmolested. Safe and sound.

I can't believe she was taken right off the street. Anger fills me and I know I am being irrational.

But I'm mad at everyone.

At the driver, who wasn't at his post.

At my girl for walking off alone. At me for not being there.

At this piece of shit I'm about to kill.

It's a waste of energy and I force myself to stop. Fact is, she is gone. Taken. He has her.

And I am going to get her back. I have to.

Fear pierces my heart, and it's sharp as a hollowed bullet.

Motherfucker just took her. Like a flower. He just plucked her from the street.

My mind is made up. I exhale and it ends in a rolling hiss.

I'm going to kill Matteo Sanchez.

There is no sanctuary for him.

Today, the absolute destruction of the Sanchez cartel has been etched in stone.

I already have my team moving to push them out of all their legal businesses.

Dozens of tips and files are being sent to the authorities. And leaks of Sanchez's involvement with drug and arms running have been sent to the local authorities.

Their putrid little existence is over.

This is their end.

They just don't know it yet.

It all starts now.

CHAPTER THIRTY-NINE-MARIA

Matteo drags me past a dirty entryway and opens a plain wood door to what looks like a storage room.

But it's an apartment. Or it would be if people lived there.

I see cardboard boxes and wood crates. There's a ceramic vase on a table with some packing straw and the thing is all cracked.

A man is digging inside, and he's removing bundles of what looks like sugar.

But it's not.

Fuck.

He's brought me to one of their safe houses, and I start to get really scared.

"Where the fuck is Zip?" Matteo asks.

"Back room," the stranger grunts.

"Call him."

The man shrugs and yells.

"ZIP!"

"*Callate!*" Matteo yells and throws something at him.

I recognize the word and I know it means shut up.

Another man comes running out of the back room and he's pulling up his pants.

"What? Matteo! Junior didn't say you were coming. What is this? A present for me?" Zip asks.

"Don't even fucking look at her. This one is mine," Matteo says, and I am almost grateful to him.

Zip looks mean and rough. He has a skeleton tattooed over his face, obscuring his features, and making him look like something out of a nightmare.

They exchange some harsh words in Spanish, and I cringe.

I have to get out of there.

The discussion is getting heated, and I inch back towards the door. I need to at least try to get out of there.

"Where the fuck do you think you're going?" Matteo grunts.

He grabs my arm, shoving me to the ground. I whimper. His fingernails cut into my skin and the floor is hard and unforgiving as my bare knees slam into it.

"Oh shit, I know you. This is the *puta* the Viper Council beat the shit out of Eduardo for! Get her out of here, man! Junior's gonna flip," Zip says.

"You don't fucking tell me what to do, man," Matteo yells, and I see he's losing his temper.

This is not good.

Matteo is volatile and crazy.

His hand is on his gun, and in the blink of an eye, he's pulled it out of his waistband and has it pressed against Zip's throat.

That's when shit gets crazy.

The doors bust open. I gasp and tears well in my eyes. It's Luc. And he has people with him.

Thank God.

My heart squeezes. He's come for me. I knew he would, but I'm still stuck somewhere between hope and disbelief.

My whole body is shaking. A mixture of fear and relief warring inside me. I want to run to him so badly, but I can't move.

Something isn't right. We are not safe yet.

Matteo swings around, waving the gun wildly.

"What the fuck, man? You! How did you find us?" Matteo screams, and he is sweating profusely.

"You're fucking done," Luc growls.

I've seen crazy before, and I see it again in Matteo's eyes.

Luc isn't holding a gun.

And when Matteo lifts his arm, brandishing his weapon, I push myself off the floor.

"LUC!" I yell.

Matteo shouts and squeezes the trigger and a loud pop, like a firecracker echoes in the room.

I fall to the floor.

I don't know what's happened, but I hear someone scream.

"MARIAAAA!"

The sound echoes in my ears as I lose consciousness.

CHAPTER FORTY-LUC

I see my woman leap from the floor just as this dead motherfucker raises his arm to shoot at me.

I see the shot go off.

I watch helplessly as Maria's body lurches backwards and crumbles to the ground as she takes the bullet meant for me.

And I stop being human in that moment.

A pain filled roar rips out of me, and I leap across the room, my hands closing around Matteo Sanchez's worthless neck.

I'm thinner than he is. But I'm strong. And I'm so fucking mad.

My fury takes us both down.

I lift his head and slam it into the floor.

The sound is harsh.

"Stop!" he says.

"Please!"

But I don't.

I can't.

The Viper is free, and all I see is red.

I want his blood on my hands. Need to see it staining the floor.

Chaos is erupting around me, but I don't care.

I slam his head against the floor once more.

It's not enough. I dig my thumbs into his eyes.

He is scratching at my shoulders, trying to get away. But he can't.

I'm straddling his chest.

I lift his head and I slam it down again.

And again.

And again.

A sick crunch echoes in the room. I hear someone yell. But I don't fucking care.

I feel liquid warmth seep between my fingers.

But I'm not finished.

I don't stop. I just keep cracking his head against the floor until it opens like a ripe melon.

When his brains are spilling from the mess, covering the fucking ground, that is when I stop.

It can't take more than a minute or two to end him.

I watch his eyes glaze over as death comes to take him to hell, and it's more time than he deserves.

Too much fucking time away from Baby Girl.

"Maria!" I yell and crawl to where she's collapsed.

"Luc," Angel runs to my side. Nico is with him.

Both are a little worse for wear, and I know they rained terror down on these maggots. But I can't do anything but call her name over and over again.

It's like I think I can fix her if I just keep saying it.

"Maria. Maria. Maria. MAARRIIAAAAAAAA!"

I roar this time, but I can't just breakdown. She needs me.

I search for the injury. My mind insists maybe it missed her.

It didn't.

I find the entry wound to the bullet she took for me in her left shoulder.

"Come on. Let them work. She needs a hospital," Nico says, shaking me, but I won't let her go.

I don't see or hear the EMTs arrive. Suddenly, they are just there.

"Sir, please. Let us help her," a woman's voice says, and I look her in the eye before I place Maria on the backboard.

"Help her. Now," I say.

Pain like I've never felt lances me as I watch them work.

She's unresponsive.

Fuck.

No.

Please.

They place pads on her chest and side.

"Clear!"

Then, they shock her.

The sound the machine makes is so damn sharp and shrill. Her body jumps and her head lolls to the side.

Nico and Angel are both holding me back. I don't even realize I am struggling until I see my own feet kicking out from under me.

They shock her again.

Her chest rises.

Thank God.

She's alive.

And that counts for something.

It counts for everything.

I know what I am, and I know what I deserve. And it is not her.

She is too good for me.

Too young.

Too pretty.

Too innocent and sweet.

But I'm also man enough to admit she is mine.

I'm not letting her go.

Not now. Not fucking ever.

She's with the surgeons now, and Angel is hustling me into a room.

"Take your fucking clothes off, man. I'm not undressing you, Luc," he says, exasperated.

I haven't uttered a single word since I talked to the surgeon.

Well, I say talk.

But it's more like threaten.

As in *she dies, you fucking die.*

I think he gets the message. But just to smooth things over, I have one of my guys send fifty grand as a donation to his kid's school's athletic fund.

"Get in there," Angel says, and he's putting my clothes into a plastic bag as I step into the shower.

"Luc, snap the fuck out of it. I need you to get washed and put on these clothes when you're done," he says, pointing to a pile of clean clothes he just set on the counter.

"Nico is with Anna. She's to be kept in the dark about all this. But he's gonna want to talk to you. So, move it."

I stare at him, but he just growls and turns on the water.

It's fucking cold. But I still make no sound.

"Don't go catatonic on me, asshole. Here," he squeezes shampoo onto my head.

"And hurry your ass up, or I'll tell Maria you asked me to wash your dick," he says.

What the fuck is wrong with him, saying shit like that at a time like this?

But it's just like Angel. And it gets me moving.

There's only one person allowed access to my body, and that's her. No one, and I mean that, no fucking one, is ever coming close to my dick again.

Just her. Only Maria.

My Baby Girl.

My love.

I scrub soap all over my hair and body.

I step into the now warm water and watch red rivers wash off my skin, spiraling down the drain.

Fuck.

I am covered in blood.

Some of it is Maria's, and that makes me want to howl like a wounded beast.

But most, I am sure, is that dead fucking pig's blood.

And that placates me.

I don't care what it takes to convince her to stay with me.

But I'm going to do it.

She took a bullet meant for me.

My heart squeezes. I never want her in danger again.

She says she loves me.

My pulse races. I love her back. And I am going to tell her as soon as she opens her beautiful almond eyes.

Maria is my other half in every single way.

She sees the madness in me, and she doesn't shy away.

She takes in the hard parts and sharp edges, and she cradles them to her breast.

So much. She does so much for me.

Soothes the rage.

Sates the hunger.

Makes the quiet more palatable.

I need her.

I will do anything for her.

Except leave her.

I will never do that.

CHAPTER FORTY-ONE-MARIA

My mouth feels like shit.

It's dry and scratchy, and I need water or something to drink. But I can't talk just yet.

I'm stuck somewhere between sleep and wake.

Flashes flit through my troubled mind.

Moments of consciousness followed by moments of cold, empty, dark.

"Easy *mija*, Mami is here," my mother's voice dances inside my ears.

"Everything looks good on her chart. We just have to wait. It's up to Mia—" I think that must be the doctor, but I don't remember.

It doesn't matter because he is being interrupted.

"Her name is Maria," a familiar voice says,

correcting the stranger, and I feel like I could cry and laugh at the same time.

Luc.

He's not hurt or worse. Matteo didn't get him.

Thank God.

I love you, Luc.

Fade to black.

I don't want to be in the dark anymore.

I don't want to be alone.

Luc.

I want him to come back.

I hate the hospital. It smells bad, and everyone is always poking and prodding me. I just want to leave.

Take me home, Luc. Just take me home.

CHAPTER FORTY-TWO-LUC

After dismissing the doctor, I say goodbye to Maria's mother and dip my chin in Joe's direction as they take their leave.

They come every day. Now that Matteo is no longer a threat, Maria's mother can visit as often as she likes.

And she has been by every day with the guards I provide and Joe. I think he has real feelings for her, and that just goes to show you, love knows no age.

It doesn't discriminate. And it can happen everywhere.

Fuck. I make love sound like a rash.

I never said I was a poet. Anyway, it's been seventy-two hours since her surgery. I haven't slept a wink.

How can I?

My sweet girl risked her life for me. I can't rest until I look into her beautiful eyes, and I tell her what she did, what it all means.

Goddamn it. Why isn't she awake?

Maria should be awake by now.

"Hey, Baby Girl, I miss you so much," I say, taking her hand in mine. "Listen to me. I need you to open your pretty eyes. Come on. Open them. Do it for me. I need to see you. Please, Maria."

I should feel ridiculous. My girl is unconscious and I'm over here begging her to wake up.

As if I could pull something like that off.

Doesn't matter. I still have to try.

Ever since she got shot, it's like the sun went black. Everything good and light has just up and disappeared.

Nico understands. He's handling the search for Sanchez Junior just fine while I stay right fucking here.

I have feelers out. It isn't like I'm dormant.

But I've been spending most of my time holding Maria's hand and reading *Dante* in the original Italian to her.

I know how she likes it when I do that while I'm wearing my glasses.

I drop my forehead to the bed, praying to whatever God might be out there, listening to bring her back to me.

And I guess they were listening, because the next thing I know, she's squeezing my hand back.

I look up, and I see her face.

"Maria? Oh, thank God. Thank fucking God. Oh, Baby Girl, I missed you so much," I tell her, and I feel like my heart might explode with emotion.

Maria's blinking her eyes, and she's trying to smile, but I can tell she's uncomfortable.

"Here," I say, and I hold a straw to her lips.

She takes a long sip and sighs.

"Luc," she whispers, after she is finished drinking.

"Hi," I tell her, brushing back her hair.

"Are you okay?" she mouths, her voice still too hoarse to make much sound.

"Yeah, I'm okay. Because of you, I'm okay," I say, and I drop a soft kiss on her lips.

"Goddamn it, Baby. You had me so worried," I say and carefully wrap her in my embrace, watchful of her injury.

"You crazy woman. You will never do anything

like that again, got it? I fucking love you so much and I almost lost you, and I just can't do that again," I tell her and I know I am rambling, but I can't stop.

It's like someone opened the floodgates and all my feelings are pouring out of my mouth.

I cup her cheeks lift my face so I can see her. Tears are streaming from her eyes, and my breath hitches and I know I am crying too.

"You love me?" she says, the last word comes out completely silent.

"Of course, I love you. How can I help but love you, my Baby Girl?"

Now, she's smiling and crying at the same time.

There is a storm raging outside the hospital room. Her eyes flick to it, and I grin.

"It's been raining since you got shot," I tell her just as a lion's roar of thunder shakes the sky.

Lightning crashes and I stare at her.

"Will they let me leave soon?" she asks.

The answer is yes. If the doctor says it's safe, of course.

But before we settle that, we have things to discuss.

"We need to talk," I tell her, taking her hands.

She looks at me, curious, and maybe a little bit wary.

"Your mother wants you to go home with her.

"What? But—"

"Let me finish. Look, I'm sorry. I'm sorry, Maria. I just can't do this—"

But before I can finish my sentence, she is shaking her head and clutching at me.

"Luc, please. I know I lied in the beginning. But I love you. We can work it out. Please, don't send me away," she says, tears in her eyes, and it is breaking my heart.

Another boom of thunder, and she gasps. But her eyes are on me.

The misery I see there is all because she thinks I am sending her away.

God, I love her so much.

I'm not saying what she thinks I'm saying. So, I clarify.

"Send you away? Baby Girl, I am not sending you away. I respectfully told your mother no."

"What? I thought you meant you were leaving me," she whispers. And I cup her cheeks and kiss her quickly.

She doesn't have the strength to do what I want to do to her. So I have to keep it short.

"It's been a rough couple of days, and I'm not good with words right now.

"Imagine that? A lawyer who's no good with words," she teases, but her eyes are still full of tears.

"Look, I'm trying to say I can't be your fucking boyfriend. I can't be somebody you can leave. I need you to belong to me and I wanna belong to you."

She gasps and covers her mouth with her hand.

But I need to see her, so I pull it down.

It's a totally domineering dick thing to do. But I can't help it.

I want nothing between us when I say this.

No more lies. No more miscommunication.

This woman is more important to me than my own life. And it's time she knows it,

"When I said I can't do this, I meant I can't do anything without you. I love you. Do you hear me? I am so fucking in love with you. So, no more boyfriend and girlfriend. And, with all due respect to your mother, you are never living with her again. You are never living anywhere but with me, you got it?"

Her big beautiful eyes are still swimming with tears even as she laughs at that.

"So, what are you saying?"

"The only thing I can say. You're going to marry me. You're going to be my wife, and I'm going to be your husband. Now, look at me with those beautiful almond eyes of yours and tell me what I already know."

"You're serious?" she asks.

As if I could be anything but.

This woman.

"Tell me you're mine. Say yes, you will marry me, Baby Girl, and make me the happiest man in the world."

"Yes. Oh, yes," she says, and I kiss her once gently before I call for Preacher to come in.

"Sign this," I tell Maria, handing her a marriage license and a change of name form.

She does without reading them.

Maria signs both forms, and my heart is pounding.

"Wait. My name is Mia though," she says, and she frowns.

She is right to frown. That name doesn't suit her.

It's not hers anymore. Back when she was Mia, she wasn't mine. So no, that's no fucking name for *my wife*.

"Nuh uh. That second form is a change of name form. You're my Maria. *Maria Batiste*, now."

Another bossy dick move, but my girl doesn't seem to mind.

That's the name she used when I met her. It's how I know her. And it is who she has become.

Mine. All fucking mine.

She smiles even wider, and a ray of light seems to wash over her face. Just like that, the sun is back out.

"Are you ready for me, Mr. Batiste?" Preacher asks and walks in the room with Nico and Angel behind him.

I pluck a rose from one of the dozens of arrangements I've had delivered to her room, and I hand it to her.

"Yeah. We're ready," I say, and I hold her other hand as Preacher marries us.

My blood brothers stand in silent witness as Preacher marries us. Maria is beaming.

And when she says I do, I feel complete for the first time in my life.

"We'll do it again with people. Have a party," I say, suddenly feeling guilty for robbing her of that in my need to bind her to me.

"This is perfect, Luc. All I want is you," she tells me.

And she's right. This is perfect.

Christ, I love her.

EPILOGUE ONE-MARIA

Getting married in a hospital room after having major surgery without even taking a shower first sounds a lot worse than it actually was.

Luc is my husband now. And I am his wife.

Even better, he says he loves me. A lot. Like all the time now.

The doctor wouldn't allow me to go home that night. In fact, it takes another week before he lets me out.

Nico said this has to all be a secret from Anna, and I have no one to share the news with except Mami.

She is a little salty about not being able to throw a big party for her only daughter, but I tell her we are going to do something big later.

Right now, I have other things on my mind. Like how freaking tired I am of being stuck in this room.

"Okay, everything is normal, and I think you are healing even faster now," the doctor says, making notes.

No shit, my body is healing faster. It wants to get home to claim my husband.

I was raised in the church, and marriage isn't real until you do the deed.

Like have sex.

I miss sex with Luc. I want it. I want it very much.

And I feel good. The bullet went clean through and as for the rest of me, I am eager to be alone with my husband.

Luc is staring at me while the doctor works, and I hear him growl when the man lifts the stethoscope to my chest.

"Just one more question," he asks, and I am still looking at Luc when he speaks.

"Have you had a bowel movement yet?"

My cheeks heat with embarrassment, and I really wish the floor would just open up and swallow me.

But it doesn't.

Anna was right. Apparently, you can't leave a hospital without pooping when you've been admitted. So, I nod my head, and when I find the courage to look up, I see Luc still watching me.

Only this time, his brows are furrowed.

I know it's silly, but I don't really want to talk about BMs with my sexy as fuck husband.

The doctor seems to get it, and he nods.

"Nothing to be embarrassed about, Mrs. Batiste. Everyone poops," the doctor says, and winks.

"Oh my God," I groan and close my eyes.

Luc is grinning now, and that's good. I thought for sure he might try to take a swing at the guy for winking at me.

"Ready?" my husband asks after I sign what feels like ten thousand more forms.

"God, yes. Please get me out of here."

"Anything for you, Baby Girl," he says, and he picks me up and carries me to his car.

I snuggle into his embrace, amazed and not by how easily he bears my weight.

Luc is strong. Like really strong. And for the first time in what feels like forever, I feel safe.

I've been running for so long. It feels great to finally be free. To not have that threat hanging over my head.

"What's that look for?" Luc asks after we're both inside the car.

He pulls out of the parking spot after double checking that I'm buckled in for safety, and I can't take my eyes off him.

"Just thinking how lucky I am," I say, honestly.

"Oh yeah, and how's that, Mrs. Batiste?"

Christ, I love it when he calls me that.

"I have you, don't I?" I tease, but I mean every word.

He turns his steel gaze to mine, and I swear my breath whooshes right out of my lungs.

He is so damn handsome.

"You got me, Baby Girl. Me and no one else for life."

"Why would I ever want anyone else?" I ask him.

"Mmm."

My quiet man hums in agreement and kisses my knuckles before placing them with his on the gearshift.

Then he drives us home, and he doesn't let go the entire way there.

I really am the luckiest woman I know.

EPILOGUE TWO-LUC

Maria conked out on the way home, and I place her down on our bed, covering her with a light throw blanket before I start heating up the pot of *pozole rojo* her mother sent over that morning courtesy of her new man, Joe Palermo.

He seems to be a permanent fixture in her life now, and she looks good. Maria's mother that is. I am thrilled for them both. Happier still that my wife is happy for them.

The pozole smells incredible and I open the containers with all the toppings one at a time as I lower the heat to simmer.

I look in on her and it's like she can feel the weight of my stare.

My body responds instantly, and I should feel like a lecher, but I don't.

She took a shower earlier this morning. But I've been banged up before and I know there is nothing like bathing in your own home after so many days of being confined to a hospital room.

"Come on," I whisper, kissing her sweetly.

She doesn't resist me. And I fucking love her ready submission.

I have the water flowing, and all I need to do is kick off my sweats and remove her pajamas.

I do both, carefully. Then, I place her on the shower stool I ordered earlier this week.

"But I can stand," Maria says, and she looks confused.

I don't speak yet. My heart is beating me to death, and words can't do this moment justice.

But when I kneel in front of her, I watch as Maria's eyes fill with heat.

"Luc. Husband," she whispers and my cock jumps.

My whole life, I didn't think I needed anyone. I didn't want to be a fool for a woman.

But I've been living one big lie.

Loving someone is not what I thought it was. It is

not weakness or poison. It's a fucking gift. And I intend to hold onto this one with both hands.

Maria is my everything.

I need her so damn much. More than I can express.

My wife is essential to me.

She is necessary.

I need to show her how I feel. So, I do. By taking care of her.

I squirt some of her soap in my hand and rub my hands along her skin. And it feels, *it feels cathartic.*

Like touching her is all the medicine I need.

"Luc," she moans.

I run my fingers along her breasts in circular motions, teasing the nipples and lifting and squeezing them.

"I'm so hungry for you," I whisper and suck one into my mouth.

"Are you sure that's not just the *pozole* whetting your appetite?" she teases.

"Nothing against your mother, Baby Girl, but her cooking's got nothing on you."

Then, I grin, biting down on the hard little cherry inside my mouth. Maria gasps, then I go back to licking and sucking.

My hands continue on their mission, settling on

her hot, dripping pussy and fuck, my wife is so wet for me.

My cock grows even harder.

I know I need to take it easy, which is why I am starting with this.

I've missed her so much.

Her taste.

Her heat.

Her submission.

I push her long legs wider, and she grabs my head, helping me reach my destination, which is between her thick, gorgeous thighs.

"Oh fuck," she whimpers.

I press my face into her sex and breathe in her scent. It's lilac and honey and hot, sweet pussy. Her fragrance makes me wild for her.

"Please, Luc," she begs.

My wife fucking begs. And I can't deny her. I wouldn't dream of it.

I swipe my tongue along her slit and her shocked gasp tells me she likes the new, bigger ball at the end of my piercing.

I grin while I lap at her again and again, feeding my tongue to her hungry cunt.

"That's it, Baby Girl," I growl as I plunge two fingers into her tight heat.

"Look at me, kneeling at your altar. You're the one I worship, Maria. And I'll prove it by praying on my knees. I'll use anything to please you. My words. My hands. My lips. My tongue. And my cock," I tell her.

I don't know where she gets that honey lilac scent that seems to surround her, but I adore it. Some of it is her soap, but it's more her than anything.

I drink it in as I press my face against her.

I love her so much.

Every freaking inch.

Her hair.

Her eyes.

Her smile.

Her neck.

The valley between her breasts.

Her soft belly and long legs.

Those thick thighs.

Her bronze skin.

She is always so damn sweet and warm. I love touching her. I love the way she feels.

This woman is everything to me.

She is so brave and honest with her feelings. Even when she was lying to me, she never lied about that.

I'm acutely aware I did nothing to deserve her. I sure as fuck did not prepare for the profundity of being with her.

Every time we've come together, I lose control.

It's always me taking her anyway I can, leading the way.

Commanding.

Desperate,

Needy.

Searching.

But this time I want my wife to know how much I feel for her. I want her to take what she wants, what she needs from me. And I am determined to tell her.

I suck her clit until I feel her pussy clamp and Maria's legs start to shake.

I'm so hard, I squeeze my balls to stave off coming on the tile like some green kid.

And Maria, well she just came, but she slides off the stool, and I catch her.

"It's been too long. I need you inside me, Husband. Now," she says, all want and need.

So fucking hot.

I lift her by her thighs and drop her right on my hard as steel cock, and warm water is raining down on us.

"That's it. Fuck me. Show me what you like. Use my body to bring your pleasure. Yes, that's it," I say.

"Luc, so close," she moans, and she is rocking, wiggling, and dropping her hot pussy right on me.

I'm seconds from coming, but I need her to go first.

"Show me. Be a good little wife and show me. Come all over this dick, Baby Girl. Right. Now," I command.

And she fucking does.

Her pussy flutters and squeezes and I start to come, spilling my load so deep inside her, I swear I can taste it when I pull her in to kiss her lips.

"You're so fucking perfect," I tell her.

"I love you, too," she replies breathlessly, a happy, dazed smile on her beautiful face.

After drying us both off, I change her wound dressing, and I carry her to bed. When I return with a tray of her mother's soup, I feed her, bite for bite.

She lifts the rose I placed on the tray.

"You're like that to me. A perfect rose," I tell her.

"You mean, you think I have thorns?" she teases.

"Yeah, but I like your thorns, Baby Girl."

"And I like your forked tongue, Viper Council," she says back.

I raise one eyebrow and take the tray away, then I wrap my hands around her throat and straddle her thighs.

"The better to eat you with, Baby Girl."

"I think you're mixing up your fairytales, Husband," she says.

But she's already squirming beneath me, and I know my wife is already soaked for me.

"Maybe, but that's because this isn't a fairytale. This is real. You and me, *us, together,* is very fucking real. And I am never letting you go," I say and crash my mouth to hers.

"Now, lay back and open your legs. This Viper's still hungry. And don't move unless I say so, or I might bite you," I warn her.

I am licking my lips as I find her clit with my tongue and a part of me is hoping she moves just so I can nibble her sweet flesh.

Fuck. Yes.

I moan when she does just that.

EPILOGUE THREE-GISELLE/ANGEL

G*iselle*

I close my phone after checking out the newest images of Nico Jr. that Anna just sent over and I will myself not to cry.

Fuck.

Everything is so fucked up. I don't know what to do anymore.

I know it's stupid and weak, but after seeing Angel with that woman plastered all over him, I had to leave.

I know we never put a label on whatever it is we've been doing.

But still.

I didn't expect to see him with another woman.

Not after that whole macho fucking thing he pulled after I sorta tossed a glass of beer in his face.

For weeks he made me believe if I didn't play along with his *me Tarzan, you Jane* bullshit, that I'd suffer the consequences.

Fine. I let myself believe it because the truth is I never expected anyone who looks like him to want anything to do with someone who looks like me.

I'm not ugly. I don't have low self-esteem. But I am a realist.

My body is super curvy and ultra thick.

There is no excuse, like I can't exercise or have some metabolic disorder.

I just like food.

And I am active. I mean I swim, I walk, I hike.

But what can I say?

My chub ain't going nowhere.

But then there is Angel.

And Angel is a physical specimen right out of some dark romance novel. He's six foot six and an easy three hundred twenty pounds of curved, spectacular, rock hard muscle.

And did I mention his face?

It's gotta be kismet or something.

His name, I mean.

Because Angel Fury looks like a certified *angel.*

He is so handsome it hurts.

The dick.

He has light eyes, excellent bone structure, and full, sinfully delicious lips.

Seriously, I just wanna sit on his face for like hours with those things.

I have.

Which makes this so fucking hard.

Of course, the woman he was with at the Den was skinny and blonde and stacked like a supermodel.

I wish I could hate her, but I don't even know her.

"Did you pick a color?" the manicurist asks, and I show her the hot pink I chose for my mani-pedi.

"Okay, this way. Would you like me to turn on the chair massage?"

"Oh God, fuck yes. Oops! Sorry, I meant to say, yes, please," I tell her, and she smiles and nods knowingly.

She turns on the water and fills the foot tub, adding a blue tablet. I sit back in the chair and close my eyes, humming low in my throat as I try to ease away the horrible month I've had with a little self-care.

I already missed out on my best friend having a

baby and I feel like a fucking cockroach. But now, Anna has moved into a beautiful house in the fucking suburbs, and I am missing it all.

Not only that, but apparently Maria has gotten herself hitched to Luc and they are talking about having an actual ceremony and reception for friends and family this fall.

I am missing everything! And all because I am a goddamned coward.

"Would you like a real massage? Your shoulders look tense," the same manicurist asks.

"Sure," I reply and nod my head.

I didn't know they did that. My eyes are still closed as I lean forward to give her room. It's Fort Lauderdale and hot as fuck, so I'm wearing a cami and a pair of booty shorts.

Just like everyone else.

Big, warm hands clasp my skin and start massaging. And my eyes fly wide open.

I know those hands.

"Don't touch me," I hiss and turn my head to find Angel, looking better than anyone has a right to, massaging my shoulders.

"Don't touch you, Koukla? Last time I saw you, you were begging for my touch, remember?" he growls.

And fuck, I squeeze my thighs together in response.

"That was before I knew you're nothing but a two-timing cheat," I reply between clenched teeth and try to shake him off.

But Angel is impossible to move. And his eyes narrow like he is super pissed.

"I think we got ourselves a misunderstanding, Koukla. But no worries. We'll get that all straightened out on the way back home."

"What are you talking about? I'm not going anywhere with you."

"Darling, you can come quietly, or you can scream. Your choice," he says, and he puts his lips right against my ear, "You know how much I like it when you scream."

Then he licks my neck, biting down hard, before backing up and handing the manicurist a couple of hundreds.

"Don't worry about your parents. I got your suitcase from your mother. She's a very nice lady. Says she's been wondering why you haven't left to see Anna. Your father, too."

"You went to the condo?" I ask, eyes wide.

"Yep. Hey, you think you can work fast?"

"Yes, sir," the manicurist replies, eyeing Angel like

he's a double shot French vanilla Frappuccino with caramel syrup and whipped cream.

"Cool. Thanks. You, uh, want me to keep massaging those shoulders, Gorgeous? Or anything else? I'm always available for you," he says, eyeing me up and down.

This prick.

I narrow my gaze.

"No thanks. You're not needed here," I say, arching one eyebrow.

I grab the remote for the chair and press the button to start the deluxe message.

Fuck this asshole.

I ignore him for the next twenty minutes. And yeah, I'm bouncing around the goddamn massage chair while my toenails are being polished, and I am waiting for him to walk away so I can text Anna or Maria, anyone who will sympathize with me.

But he just stands there. Watching me.

Stupid cheating jerk.

I try to close my eyes to block him out.

Two-timing shithead.

I fucking earned this pedicure and I'm going to goddamn enjoy it

Even if I look like a bag of Jello.

Angel

I'm not made for serious relationships, but something about this woman won't let me leave her alone.

Giselle Vega.

The one who ran away. *Literally.*

I call her Koukla. It means *doll* or *little doll,* which is how I think of Giselle.

She's short.

Much shorter than me.

And she's beautiful.

Hauntingly so.

She's got this body that just won't quit. And her mouth. Her fucking mouth drives me insane.

We were messing around for a little while, and I thought we were good.

But something happened, and I don't know what. Giselle ran, and I tried to stay away.

Really, I did.

I'm not the kinda guy who chases women.

But I'm chasing her. I just can't help it.

I watch my little doll bouncing around in that

massage chair and it's all I can do not to toss her over my shoulder.

I'm not ruling it out yet.

She can spout all the pitiful lies she wants about not needing me or wanting me.

But I feel something every time we're near one another.

And she feels it too.

Whether or not she wants to admit it.

The massage chair finally stops and Giselle opens her eyes and her gaze catches mine.

"Ready, Koukla?"

But I don't wait for an answer. I just pick her up and toss her over my shoulder.

"Angel!" she says and hits my back.

It's cute.

"Knock it off, Baby Doll, or this ride is gonna be a lot messier than you want," I say and spank her juicy ass.

She stills immediately and I smirk.

This is gonna be fun.

Married life is everything I never knew it could be.

Or maybe that's just because I am married to the sexiest, most loving woman I know.

Chances are, it's the latter.

I grin over my tumbler of Whiskey Neat and watch Maria as she turns the pages of the new Z. Wolff novel she's reading.

She started a little book club with Giselle and Anna, and from what I understand, each month one of them picks a book for them to read and discuss over wine and chocolate.

The get-togethers have been hard since Giselle fled to her parents' condo in Florida, but Angel recently corrected that.

Big fucker flew down there and brought her back here. *Where she belongs*—his words, not mine.

It's nice to know I'm not the only idiot who took a while to get the girl of my dreams. But I got her now and I am never letting go.

My phone pings and I look down.

This is big news. We got him.

Sanchez Junior.

Maria is looking right at me when I lift my head.

"You have to go?"

"Yeah, Baby Girl. I have to go."

She stands and walks over to me, winding her arms around my neck. She pulls me down for a kiss and I don't even try to pretend I don't want her to do it.

I always want her to touch me.

I have to admit, for a woman who remained virginal until I got my hands on her, Maria is the most exciting lover I have ever had. She is simply incomparable.

Far as I'm concerned, there were no other women before her. Any experiences I had were just lessons, so I could please her.

And I work very fucking hard to please her.

She deserves it. And she gives it back to me tenfold.

"Come back to me in one piece, Husband," she says, and I nod.

"Always."

"Good. I got a new delivery from *Kisses by Kylie* today," she tells me, and right away my dick gets hard.

The designer lingerie label has quickly become a favorite.

"Did the panties come?"

She grins and nods her head, and for the first time ever, I seriously consider blowing Nico off.

"Go do your thing. I'll be waiting here when you're finished," she says, and licks a trail up my neck to my earlobe, sucking my earring into her mouth.

My entire body quivers. I have to go. But I know I'll be focused and fast just so I can come home.

To her.

I squeeze her ass and drive my tongue down her throat and Maria moans, submitting to me in the way she knows I need her to.

"I'll be back soon."

"I'll be ready," she replies.

"I love you, Husband."

"And I love you, Wife."

.   .   .

T*he end.*

These wild billionaire playboys are used to getting their way...

There isn't much money can't buy, especially when it comes to pleasure. But can these curvy women tame these billionaire beasts and win their love? Or will their souls be sucked into oblivion by the wanton bliss their bodies crave more and more with every surrender?

Each of our heroes wears a mask on the outside to face the world, but his disguise comes off when he runs into the one female who makes his blood run hot. Need and possessive passion abound in these books, but our heroes know only one way to control their desires.

Will they f*ck the feeling they see as weakness out of their systems, or will their needs only grow more wild with every touch, kiss, and plunge into ecstasy with the object of his affections?

Our Billionaire Heroes

Adrik Volkov
Marat Volkov
Josef Aziz
Andres Ramirez

Content Warnings

**This series has profanity, graphic, steamy scenes, violence, homicide, talk of deceased relatives, references to sexual assault and abuse (not by the MCs), mention of domestic violence (not perpetrated by MCs), mention of suicide, alcohol consumption, misogyny (not the MCs), questionable morals, hurtful past, manipulations, fake relationships, lies, revenge, forced marriages, very bad decisions, and romantic obsessions that may be unhealthy. The FMC works at a shelter for abused women and children.*

This is a fictional story with fictional characters. This is not real life.

Always take care of your mental, emotional, and physical self because you are important.

P.S.

For those who asked Adrik is pronounced Ade-drick and Marat is Meh-Rut. Happy reading!

ALSO BY C.D. GORRI

<u>Contemporary Romance Books:</u>

<u>Cherry On Top Tales</u>

Her Yule His Log

His Carrot Her Muffin

Her Chocolate His Bar

His Pickle Her Jam

<u>Wild Billionaire Romance</u>

His Wild Obsession

His Wild Temptation

His Wild Seduction

His Wild Attraction

<u>Jersey Bad Boys</u>

Merciful Lies

Devious Lies

Pitiful Lies

***

<u>Paranormal Romance Books:</u>

<u>Macconwood Pack Novel Series:</u>

<u>Macconwood Pack Tales Series:</u>

The Falk Clan Tales:

The Bear Claw Tales:

The Barvale Clan Tales:

Barvale Holiday Tales:

Purely Paranormal Romance Books:

The Wardens of Terra:

The Maverick Pride Tales:

Dire Wolf Mates:

Wyvern Protection Unit:

Jersey Sure Shifters/EveL Worlds:

The Guardians of Chaos:

Twice Mated Tales

Hearts of Stone Series

Moongate Island Tales

Mated in Hope Falls

Speed Dating with the Denizens of the Underworld

Hungry Fur Love

Island Stripe Pride

NYC Shifter Tales

A Howlin' Good Fairytale Retelling

Witch Shifter Clan

Young Adult/Urban Fantasy Books

The Grazi Kelly Novel Series

The Angela Tanner Files

G'Witches Magical Mysteries Series

Co-written with P. Mattern

Witches of Westwood Academy

with Gina Kincade

Blackthorn Academy For Supernaturals

**Be sure to check out my BUY DIRECT BUNDLES and get 30% off when you buy available only my website.*

Click here for The Official C.D. Gorri Reading List - free download

Coming Soon

Motley Crewd Shifters

Mergers & Acquisitions

ABOUT THE AUTHOR

USA Today Bestselling author C.D. Gorri writes paranormal and contemporary romance and urban fantasy books with plenty of steam and humor.

Join her mailing list here: https://www.cdgorri.com/newsletter

An avid reader with a profound love for books and literature, she is usually found with a book in hand. C.D. lives in her home state, New Jersey, where many of her characters and stories are based. Her tales are fast-paced yet detailed with satisfying conclusions. If you enjoy powerful heroines and loyal heroes who face relatable problems in supernatural settings, journey into the Grazi Kelly Universe today.

You will find sassy, curvy heroines and sexy, love-driven heroes who find their HEAs between the pages.

Wolves, Bears, Dragons, Tigers, Witches, Vampires, and tons more Shifters and supernatural creatures dwell within her paranormal works. The most important thing is every mate in this universe is fated, loyal, and true lovers always get their happily-ever-afters.

In her contemporary works, you will find fiercely possessive men and the smart, confident, curvy women they are crazy about. As always, the HEA is between the pages.

Thank you and happy reading!
del mare alla stella,
C.D. Gorri

http://www.cdgorri.com
https://www.facebook.com/Cdgorribooks
https://www.bookbub.com/authors/c-d-gorri
https://twitter.com/cgor22
https://instagram.com/cdgorri/
https://www.goodreads.com/cdgorri
https://www.tiktok.com/@cdgorriauthor